THE PINK PANTHER
Junior Novel™

THE PINK PANTHER

Junior Novel

A Novel Based on the Major Motion Picture

Based on the Screenplay by Len Blum and Steve Martin
and Story by Len Blum and Michael Saltzman
Adapted by Kirsten Larsen

an imprint of
HYPERION BOOKS FOR CHILDREN
New York

At the time of printing, we worked from the most current script available, but some scenes may have changed in postproduction.

Printed in the United States of America
First Edition
3 5 7 9 10 8 6 4 2
ISBN 0-7868-3736-5

This book is set in 13/18 New Baskerville.
Book design by Roberta Pressel

www.pinkpantherthemovie.com

Chapter 1

One night, in a small apartment in Paris, the famous Inspector Clouseau sat at his new computer, working on some top secret correspondence. Outside his window, the lights of the city twinkled in the night. In the distance, the brightly lit Eiffel Tower rose majestically against the sky.

"To send an e-mail," Clouseau read aloud from the computer's instruction manual, *"type in the name of the recipient."*

Inspector Clouseau looked down at the computer keyboard. Painstakingly, he typed in (BRITNEY SPEARS).

"Now," he read out loud, *"type a massage in the*

1

space marked 'massage.'" Clouseau looked at the computer screen. "Ah. A *massage*," he repeated.

DEAR BRITNEY, he typed into the message space. I AM A BIG FAN. I THINK YOU ARE *BAD*. I HOPE YOU ENJOY MY MASSAGE. I HOPE YOU WILL MASSAGE ME BACK.

"When you are ready to send the massage, press SEND," he read from the manual.

I use the moose, Clouseau said to himself, fumbling with the computer mouse. I click but do not drag the button that says SEND.

Clouseau clicked the SEND button. The computer whirred. It began to grind like a garbage disposal. Suddenly, all the lights in Clouseau's apartment went out.

Across the street, too, in a restaurant packed with people eating and drinking, the lights went out. A waiter carrying plates of food stopped and scowled. He knew exactly what the problem was.

"Clouseau . . ." he snarled.

At the same moment, on the other side of the city, the spotlights shining on the Eiffel

Tower suddenly went off.

"Clouseau," muttered a nearby vendor.

Meanwhile, on the other side of the Atlantic Ocean, a television director was standing in a newsroom, watching an important broadcast. Just as the TV announcer declared, "And now, ladies and gentlemen, the President of the United States—" every single TV screen in the newsroom went blank.

"Clouseau," howled the TV director.

Across the globe, in a vast, windswept desert, a group of Bedouins were huddled together in a tent, eating their dinner by the light of a single candle. Suddenly, the candle went out.

"Clouseau," grumbled one of the Bedouins.

Jacques Clouseau's was the most famous name in the history of French law enforcement. His ineptitude was staggering. His bumbling was beyond belief. His accent was just plain silly. In short, he was absolutely the worst police officer the world had ever seen.

No one knew this better than Charles

Dreyfus, the chief inspector of the French national police. Dreyfus rued the day that he had ever heard the name Clouseau—although it was difficult to say *which* day that actually was. In his years as chief inspector, Dreyfus had heard many stories about officers working in the field. And there had been many, many stories about Clouseau.

Clouseau had begun his career as a third-class officer, working in a little village outside of Paris.

Even in the early days, his incompetence was unparalleled. One example of his bungling occurred when he was called in to investigate some missing meat that a hot-dog vendor had reported stolen.

With two gendarmes along to assist, Clouseau went to question the victim of the crime.

"Oh, thank goodness you are here!" the hot-dog vendor said when he saw Clouseau and the policemen approach. "I have two dozen missing hot dogs!"

"Why two dozen?" Clouseau asked suspiciously, pointing the riding crop he always carried at the vendor's nose.

The vendor looked confused. "I . . . I don't know," he replied.

"Good," Clouseau said. "If you had known, you would be a suspect."

"They come twelve to a package," the vendor's assistant volunteered.

Clouseau whipped around to face him. "You are a suspect! Into the van!" he ordered, pointing to the police paddy wagon that was parked nearby.

As a gendarme hustled the assistant away, the vendor complained, "Someone is stealing my hot dogs."

"A clear violation of statute 209A," the other gendarme piped up.

Clouseau gave him a disdainful look. *"Statute 209, part A: a restaurant serving raw meat must be licensed for such; a brasserie serving cheese must also purchase an equal volume of ice; no café can have tables less than three feet from the boulevard,"* he recited. *"Sections B and C repealed in 1897. Section D: all streets bordering an abattoir shall be outfitted with a blood gutter terminating in a municipal sewer or licensed drainage ditch.*

"So," Clouseau concluded snappishly, "I assume you mean statute 212C: *unlawful to steal hot dogs.*"

The gendarme hung his head.

"Now," Clouseau said, turning back to the vendor, "tell me a little bit about the hot-dog business."

"Well, someone will come up to me and say, 'I would like a hot dog,'" the vendor explained.

"And then?" asked Clouseau.

"I sell them the hot dog."

"Hmmm." Clouseau tapped his riding crop thoughtfully against his palm. "Let me get this correct. You sell someone a hot dog. . . ."

The vendor nodded. "Yes."

"And then he asks for the hot dog?" Clouseau said.

"No. They ask for the hot dog, and *then* I sell it to him," the vendor said, correcting him.

Clouseau thought about this for a moment. "Clever," he said at last. "Congratulations, monsieur. You are in a complicated business."

Clouseau looked around the outdoor courtyard, where the vendor's cart was parked. Several people were sitting at small tables, eating their lunch. "Well," he said, "obviously the perpetrator of the crime is here...lurking...somewhere...."

"Everyone! Up against zuh well!" Clouseau shouted suddenly.

The people all looked at one another, wondering if they'd heard correctly.

"Up against zuh well!" Clouseau commanded.

The patrons all sprang from their chairs and ran to an old stone well in the center of the courtyard.

"What are they doing?" Clouseau asked the gendarme.

"You said, 'up against the well,'" the gendarme replied.

"I said, 'zuh *well*'! Not 'zuh *well*'!" Clouseau cried. He pointed to the courtyard wall.

The people moved over to the wall and placed their hands against it. One by one, Clouseau began to frisk the "suspects."

By the time Clouseau was done, he had arrested every man in the courtyard. He drove back to police headquarters, confident that he had found the criminals who had stolen the vendor's hot dogs.

This was only one of the many idiotic mistakes Clouseau had made that had reached the ears of Chief Inspector Dreyfus. Needless to say, Clouseau didn't qualify for even the smallest advancement. Clouseau might have stayed in the little village forever, terrorizing its citizens with his stupidity, but then came the semifinal game of the international soccer championships. And everything changed.

Chapter 2

On the day of the semifinal game, the stands of the French National Soccer Stadium were packed. France and China were competing in the world soccer championships. Fans from both countries cheered wildly as the members of their teams lined up on the field.

In the French VIP box, surrounded by secret-service men, the French president and the minister of justice cheered, too. Chief Inspector Dreyfus sat next to them, his eyes glazed over with boredom. He could not have cared less about soccer. But he knew it was a great honor to be invited to watch the game with the president. And Dreyfus liked honors.

Dreyfus had just been nominated for the Medal of Honor, France's most distinguished award. It was the seventh time he had received a nomination. Every other time, the award had gone to someone else. But this year, Dreyfus vowed, things would be different.

"And now," the stadium announcer declared, interrupting Dreyfus's thoughts, "the coach of France—Yves Gluant!"

The crowd sent up a deafening cheer as the handsome coach stepped out of the French team's box. Turning to the packed stands, he raised his fist, on which sat a huge, glittering pink diamond. The French fans went wild. The diamond was called the Pink Panther, named for the tiny flaw at its center, in the shape of a leaping panther. It was the most famous jewel in all of Europe. In raising his diamond ring to the crowd, Gluant was declaring victory for the French team.

At last, Gluant lowered his hand and began to walk toward his players, who were lined up on the field. As the coach approached, Bizu, the team's star striker, glared at him from beneath a wild shock of black hair. The look Bizu gave Gluant was one of pure hatred.

Gluant didn't appear to notice. He continued walking until he reached the front row of the stadium, where Xania, a stunningly beautiful pop star, sat surrounded by security guards and fans. Gluant and Xania were having a famously stormy affair. Every day reports of their fights appeared in the nation's tabloids.

Xania stood up when she saw Gluant. He walked up to her, took her hands, and murmured something to her. Then, with the entire stadium watching, he pulled her close and passionately kissed her.

The fans cheered again. On the field, Bizu scowled, his eyes flashing with jealousy.

At last, the game began. It was a tense match, with China scoring a goal for every goal scored by the French. By the end of regulation time, the score was tied, and the game went into sudden-death overtime.

The fans were on the edges of their seats. A

Chinese forward made a shot that nearly won the game. But the French goalie was too quick and dived in for a desperate save.

Then, with a minute left on the clock, Gluant gestured from the sidelines. To the astonishment of everyone in the stadium, he sent a young player named Jacquard to the forward position, and signaled for the great Bizu to come off the field.

Bizu was furious. Red-faced, he charged up to the coach and began to scream at him. When Gluant replied, Bizu punched him.

At once a fight broke out. The French trainer and assistant coach tried to pry Bizu's hands from Gluant's neck as the referee ran in from the field.

But Gluant waved the referee off, signaling for the game to continue. At the referee's whistle, someone from the Chinese team threw the ball in from the sidelines. A French player intercepted and sent the ball up the field in a long, high kick. As the ball arced through the air, Jacquard, the young forward, charged after it.

The crowd held its breath. Jacquard leaped into the air to head the ball into the Chinese goal. But suddenly he realized the ball was coming down *behind* him. And then, a miracle: Jacquard flipped forward in the air and kicked the ball into the net with the back of his heel.

The stadium exploded, the fans screaming in ecstasy. The French president, the minister of justice, and the secret-service men all leaped to their feet, cheering.

With fists raised in victory, Jacquard ran to embrace the French coach. A mob of other coaches, players, photographers, and crazed fans surged onto the field to congratulate them.

Then, suddenly, in front of a stadium full of cheering fans, Gluant collapsed—dead.

And the Pink Panther, the most famous jewel in all of Europe, disappeared.

The next day, sensational headlines were splashed across newspapers all over Europe:

FOOTBALL GENIUS MURDERED!

KILLED FOR DIAMOND RING!

PINK PANTHER RING STOLEN BY KILLER!

It was the most important moment in Chief Inspector Dreyfus's life.

Later, as he stood in his office getting fitted in his tuxedo, Dreyfus exclaimed, "The Medal of Honor ceremony is only three weeks away!" All around him, blown-up photographs of the crime scene and the Pink Panther diamond were pinned to his office walls.

"You'll get it this time," replied Agent Renard. He was the deputy chief of the French police and Dreyfus's right-hand man.

"Don't patronize me," Dreyfus snapped. "It's a disaster. If I officially take the Gluant case but don't find the killer before the ceremony, I'll look like a jerk, and the medal will go to someone else. Again."

Renard nodded sympathetically.

"If I assign the case to someone else and *he* finds the killer," Dreyfus went on, "*he'll* get the medal. It's a nightmare! I should win the Medal of Honor. It would glorify France for me to win. . . ."

As he spoke, Dreyfus's eyes fell upon the

portrait of Charles de Gaulle, the former French president. He paused and stared at the picture. An idea was slowly forming in his mind.

"My God," he said. "I know what we need for the Gluant murder."

"What?" asked Renard.

"An incompetent." Dreyfus turned to face Renard. "An unimaginative, by-the-book, low-level incompetent, who'll plod along, with the media watching his every step, but who will get nowhere."

Dreyfus began to pace around the room.

"And while he's getting nowhere," he continued with excitement, "I'll put together the finest investigators in France, and work around the clock, in secrecy, to hunt down the killer. Then, the medal will be mine."

He paused before the enlarged photo of the Pink Panther diamond, then turned back to Renard. "And I think I know the perfect man for the job. Find him and bring him to Paris. His name is Clouseau."

Chapter 3

A few days later Inspector Clouseau was on his way to Paris. In the little village, a huge crowd gathered to see him off. Clouseau shook their hands, then climbed into his tiny red car and drove away.

The moment Clouseau's car was out of sight, the townspeople began to clap their hands and jump up and down, rejoicing. How long they had dreamed of this day! "*Bon voyage*, Clouseau!" they cried. "And good riddance!"

Clouseau drove down the country road, looking at a map of France. After much searching, he finally located the dot labeled "Paris." He was pleased to see that it wasn't far at all.

A few hours later Clouseau arrived in Paris. He drove past the famous Arc de Triomphe and along the sparkling river Seine. Clouseau didn't notice. He passed the Eiffel Tower. Again, Clouseau saw nothing. He followed the street as it curved around a traffic circle. . . .

. . . And drove right back out of Paris the way he'd come in.

Several miles out of town, on a country road, Clouseau stopped the car. He'd been driving for hours, he thought, frustrated, and yet he hadn't seen a single sign for Paris!

Spotting a gas station, Clouseau approached the attendant and asked him how to get to Paris. The man stared at him for a moment, then pointed in the direction from which Clouseau had come.

Later that day, Clouseau finally pulled up to the Palais de la Justice, the impressive building that housed France's ministry of justice.

Quelle fortune! Clouseau thought, spotting a parking space right in front.

He began to maneuver his tiny car into the

wide spot. Lurching forward and backward—even sideways—he ripped the bumpers off the cars in front of and behind him. At last, the car was parked to his satisfaction.

Meanwhile, inside the Palais de la Justice, Inspector Dreyfus had assembled a team of top secret agents and was briefing them on the Gluant murder.

"Gluant was killed by a poisonous dart of Chinese origin," Dreyfus explained, pointing to an enlarged photo of Gluant just after he was murdered. A tiny dart was lodged in the coach's neck.

"Sophisticated in design, but easy to use. It could have been delivered by hand from anyone within arm's length. . . ." Dreyfus quickly reviewed the list of the people who had been standing close to Gluant at the moment of his murder: players, staff, fans, photographers, Bizu, Xania.

"Or," he continued, "it could have been shot from a tube—even a simple drinking straw—with accuracy up to thirty feet." Gluant had been standing near a section of the stadium where several angry Chinese fans were sitting. It could have been any one of them.

"Renard," said Dreyfus, turning to the deputy chief, "your team will analyze the television footage, identify each person in the kill zone, and investigate them."

"Yes, Chief Inspector!" exclaimed Renard.

"You will also locate every firm in China making darts and get their order books for the last five years," Dreyfus added.

"It will be done," said Renard.

"Corbeille," Dreyfus said, turning to another agent, "put together Gluant's schedule as far back as you can. Day by day. Everything he did."

"Yes, Chief Inspector!" said Corbeille.

"Savard," he told another agent, "your team will investigate anyone Gluant had dealings with, anyone he owed money to, anyone who had a grudge against him. If he bullied a child in kindergarten, I want to know where that child was at the time of the murder. Is that clear?"

"Yes, Chief Inspector!" said Savard.

At that moment, Inspector Clouseau arrived in the waiting room just outside Dreyfus's office. Entering, he saw Dreyfus's secretary, a pretty woman with glasses, standing on her desk and trying to hang a picture of Dreyfus on the wall.

Clouseau marched over to the desk, until his eyes were at the level of the secretary's knees. "Good morning, mademoiselle," he said, removing his blue policeman's cap.

"I'll be right with you," said the secretary, whose name was Nicole. "The minister of justice sent around a new picture of himself. . . ." She struggled with the large portrait. "But it was bigger than Chief Inspector Dreyfus's picture. So the chief inspector had a larger one made."

At last Nicole managed to get the picture onto the hook. She stepped back on her desk to look at it. "You'll find that Paris can be a very political place," she added.

"Ah, yes, politics . . . where greed wears the mask of morality," Clouseau replied sagely.

"That's good," said Nicole. "Did you say that?"

Clouseau looked around the room. Seeing no one else there, he replied, "Yes, I did."

Nicole smiled. Coming to the edge of the desk, she held out her hand so that Clouseau could help her down.

"Your hand?" Nicole said, when he didn't offer it.

Clouseau looked at her hand. "I'm afraid that is *your* hand," he corrected her.

"Yes," said Nicole. "But if you take it, you could help me down."

"Of course," said Clouseau. But rather than taking her hand, Clouseau reached up both his arms. Charmed, Nicole lowered herself from the desk. But she accidentally ended up with her legs on Clouseau's shoulders. For a moment, they staggered around, trying to get their balance.

Just then, Agent Savard stepped into the reception area. To his surprise, he saw Clouseau leaning against a wall with Nicole sitting on his shoulders.

"The Chief Inspector will see you now,"

Savard told Clouseau abruptly. He turned on his heel and went back into Dreyfus's office.

"He is coming in," Savard informed the chief inspector.

"Can you tell anything about him?" Dreyfus asked.

Savard leaned in close to Dreyfus. "He has quite a way with the ladies!" he whispered.

"Officer Jacques Clouseau! Gendarme third class!" Clouseau declared, entering with a crisp salute. He whipped open his wallet to show his badge . . . which flew off and got stuck in the chief inspector's chest. Dreyfus grimaced in pain.

"Sorry." Clouseau hurried over to pluck his badge from Dreyfus's pectoral muscle. "That must have hurt."

Dreyfus frowned. "The reason why we called you here . . ." he began.

"YES," Clouseau suddenly shouted at top volume. "IT'S VERY PLEASANT WEATHER WE'RE HAVING. I HOPE THE WEATHER CONTINUES. . . ."

Dreyfus stared at him, baffled. Clouseau gave him a thumbs-up, then began to search the room for tiny recording devices. Moving to the window curtains, he swept them dramatically aside.

"The area is secure," Clouseau declared finally, satisfied that there was no one else in the room.

"Clouseau," Dreyfus said, "I've reviewed your record, and it is my opinion that your talents merit greater responsibility than you've had to this point."

"Yes." Clouseau nodded. "I have been wondering how long it would take for stories of my expertise to reach Paris."

"I've decided to promote you to inspector, the highest rank of police officer in the republic," Dreyfus told him.

"Inspector? Of the French national police?" Clouseau asked. He had expected a promotion, but not one as grand as this.

"Yes," said Dreyfus calmly, hiding a smile. "Your first case will be the Gluant murder and the theft of the Pink Panther diamond."

"I am honored," Clouseau said with a little bow.

Dreyfus took out an official certificate. "Jacques Clouseau, with the power invested in me, I hereby appoint you a full inspector of the national police." Pulling a pen from his shirt pocket, he signed the document. "Here, take my pen," Dreyfus said, passing it to Clouseau so that he could sign, too.

"Well!" Clouseau said, impressed. "Thank you. One does not often see the traditional French fountain pen." He signed the document, then the placed expensive pen in his pocket. "I will cherish this forever," he told Dreyfus.

Dreyfus frowned. "It is not a gift," he told Clouseau. "It was given to me by the mayor."

"Well then, I cannot accept this," Clouseau said gallantly. He returned the pen to Dreyfus's shirt pocket.

"Where was I?" Dreyfus asked, once he had his pen back.

"Basically, right where you are now," said Clouseau. "Maybe a few steps back."

"The press conference . . ." Renard reminded Dreyfus.

"Yes. In a few minutes there will be a press conference in the lobby to introduce you to the media," Dreyfus told Clouseau.

As he spoke, a large black ink stain began to spread around his shirt pocket. Clouseau noticed it. His eyes widened.

"We'll meet you there. And, Clouseau," Dreyfus added. "Good luck."

"Uh . . . where is the press conference?" Clouseau asked. Eyeing the ink stain, Clouseau backed out toward the door. Just then, an intricate arch over the doorway caught his eye.

"One does not often see authentic eighteenth-century filigree," Clouseau said admiringly, reaching up and fingering the delicate design. "It is so finely done. To think this has been here for three hundred years. . . ."

As he spoke, Clouseau slowly pulled the antique filigree away from the doorway. He stared at it for a moment, then leaned it against the floor.

"It looks good anywhere," he added.

On his way out the door, Clouseau yanked a curtain aside. The curtain rod crashed down. "The area is secure," he announced.

"Yes," Dreyfus said, watching Clouseau leave, "I think we've found our man."

Then, noticing a dampish sensation near his shirt pocket, he turned to Renard. "Why do I feel wet?" he asked.

Chapter 4

The lobby of the Palais de la Justice was packed with TV news crews. Reporters and cameras swarmed around the base of a raised platform, where Dreyfus stood speaking into a microphone.

" . . . A man brought in specifically for this case," Dreyfus explained to the press, "Inspector Jacques Clouseau."

As Clouseau stepped forward, the reporters shouted questions at him. Clouseau looked around, then pointed to an attractive woman who was waving her hand in the air.

"What is your method of investigation, Inspector?" the woman reporter asked.

"Starting with an initial premise, I deduce certain other facts," he replied. "Any other questions?"

Several other reporters raised their hands.

Clouseau looked back at the pretty woman. "Do you have another question?" he asked her.

"Yes," she said.

"Would you mind raising your hand, then?" he asked.

The reporter raised her hand. "Yes?" Clouseau asked.

"And what is your initial premise?" the reporter wanted to know.

"That Gluant did not want to be killed," Clouseau replied confidently. "Everything else follows like liquid mercury flowing down . . ." Clouseau paused, wondering what mercury might flow down. ". . . A sloping . . . thing," he finished lamely.

"How long do you think it will take to find the killer?" the reporter asked.

Clouseau frowned. "I'm sorry, would you mind raising your hand again?" he asked rather apologetically. "These rules . . ."

The woman raised her hand.

"Thank you," said Clouseau. "The killer right now is being surrounded by a web of deduction, forensic science, and the latest in technology, such as two-way radios."

Behind Clouseau on the platform, Dreyfus leaned toward Renard. "Assign a man to be his driver and report on his whereabouts," he murmured.

"What kind of man?" asked Renard.

"A man who follows orders and doesn't ask questions," said Dreyfus.

Back in the media mob, a male reporter finally had the floor. "Do you know if the killer was a man or a woman?" he asked Clouseau.

"Of course I know that!" Clouseau snapped. "What else is there? A kitten?"

"Do you think it's possible that the killer could be watching you right now?" a third reporter asked.

"Well, if I were the killer, I would certainly be watching . . . and possibly taping it for later playback, because you know, it's a big deal to be talked about on TV," Clouseau replied. "And I have a message for the killer. . . ."

Clouseau turned and looked straight into the TV cameras. "There is no place you can hide," he declared, "no place you cannot be seen. *Killer, I will find you!* Because I am a servant of our nation . . . because justice is justice . . . and because France is France!"

Clouseau saluted the cameras. The room filled up with bright flashes of light as photographers snapped his picture. The policemen stationed around the lobby cheered.

Behind Clouseau, Dreyfus scowled. He didn't like the amount of attention Clouseau was getting. Not one bit.

Later that day, Clouseau was shown to his new office in the Palais de la Justice. When he entered, he found Nicole standing by his desk, holding an armload of files.

"*Bonjour*, Nicole," said Clouseau.

"This is your new office," Nicole told him.

"You should probably start by going through these files."

Clouseau motioned for her to be quiet. He glanced suspiciously around the room, pulling aside the curtains to make sure no one was behind them. Peering at a lampshade, he spotted a wire inside.

"IT IS NICE WEATHER WE'RE HAVING," Clouseau shouted, holding up the wire to show Nicole that the lamp was bugged. "I HOPE IT STAYS THIS PLEASANT."

He pulled out his pocketknife and cut the wire. *Zzzzzzt!* An electric current knocked Clouseau off his feet, and the light went out.

"The area is secure," Clouseau said when he'd recovered.

"When you are done with these files, I will bring you more files from the file cabinet, and I will refile the files, but you should probably look at these files," Nicole explained.

As she spoke, Clouseau examined his new office. When he came upon an antique wooden globe resting on a stand, he gave it a little spin.

What fun! Clouseau thought. He started to spin the globe faster and faster.

Suddenly, the globe spun off its stand and rolled out the open office door. Nicole and Clouseau hurried to the doorway and watched as the globe rolled down the stairs. Then it went on to bounce down the marble front steps of the Palais de la Justice. Leaning out the window, they saw it roll away down the street.

"That globe was a hundred years old," Nicole told Clouseau.

Clouseau sighed. "What a relief," he exclaimed, "to have ruined a new globe. . . ."

Returning to his desk, Clouseau plucked a hair from his head. He carefully placed it in his top drawer, then sat back, pleased with his cleverness. If the hair were disturbed, he would know that someone had tampered with his desk.

"Being an inspector, you'll need new clothes," Nicole told him. "If you like, I can take your measurements and have some things sent over."

"Very good," Clouseau replied.

He removed his coat. Nicole took out a tape measure and began to measure his arms.

"Perhaps you could loosen your belt so I can measure your waist," Nicole suggested.

"Of course." Just as Clouseau began to undo his belt buckle, there was a knock at the door. The door opened, and a man with broad shoulders and an eager smile stepped into the room.

But he stopped when he saw Clouseau with his belt in his hands.

The man glanced at Nicole. "Maybe I should come back later," he replied uncomfortably.

"Nonsense," said Clouseau. "We'll be done in a minute."

Reluctantly, the man entered the office and took a seat. A moment later, Nicole rose to her feet.

"Well, that takes care of that," she said. "And welcome to Paris."

The man watched as Nicole left Clouseau's office. "Your secretary?" he asked.

"The Chief Inspector's. And you are. . . ?" Clouseau asked.

"Gilbert Ponton," the man said, introducing himself. "Detective second class. I've been assigned to work with you."

"And what qualifications do you have for police work?" Clouseau wondered.

"My family has done police work in Paris for nine generations," Ponton told him.

"And before that?"

"We were policemen in the surrounding areas for two hundred years," said Ponton.

"And before that?"

"Immigrants from various countries around Europe, all involved in police work," Ponton replied.

"And before that?"

"I don't know," Ponton admitted.

"So," said Clouseau, "you are a little lamb who came to Clouseau to learn. Gilbert Ponton, I vow to teach you everything I know about policemanship. Now . . ." Clouseau rose from his chair. "Let us catch a killer."

Chapter 5

Following Dreyfus's orders, Renard had collected tapes of the France-China soccer match from every news crew that had been at the game. Now the team of secret agents sat in Dreyfus's office, reviewing the footage of Gluant's death.

On a video screen, Jacquard ran from the field to embrace Gluant as a mob of people swarmed in to congratulate them. When Gluant collapsed, the camera pulled back, revealing the crowd in the stands.

"Freeze it," Dreyfus ordered. As the image paused, he used a pointer to highlight a group of angry Chinese faces in the upper-right-hand corner of the television screen.

"The Chinese VIP box," he explained. "Right at the edge of the kill zone. The poison was Chinese. Was Gluant ever in China?"

"Three years ago he took a group of French stars there for some exhibition games," Agent Corbeille reported.

Dreyfus nodded thoughtfully. "It's a bit early to be certain, but something tells me the killer is Chinese. Corbeille, get on the next flight to Beijing. Find out what Gluant did there, where he went, who he saw. Pacquette," he said, turning to another agent, "I want a dossier on every man in that box. Go!"

As the agents scurried off, Renard approached Dreyfus. "Ponton just called," he replied. "Seems your man Clouseau is getting nowhere."

Dreyfus's eyes narrowed. "Good," he said.

Meanwhile, Clouseau and Ponton were on their way to question their first suspect. As they walked down the street, Clouseau cast doubtful glances in his partner's direction. After a while, Ponton began to feel uncomfortable.

"I'm going to be frank," Clouseau said at last. "Since you are only a detective second class, your senses may not be as sharp as my own. As I do not want a partner who makes me duller, I have in mind a way to keep you as sharp as possible."

"What is that?" asked Ponton.

"Intermittently and without warning, I will attack you—whenever and wherever it is least expected. In this way, I will keep you vigilant, alert, and ready for the unexpected," Clouseau explained. "Agreed?"

"All right," said Ponton.

They continued walking for a few paces. Suddenly, Clouseau raised his hand.

Wham! Ponton punched him in the face.

Soon, Clouseau and Ponton arrived at a building marked ALTERMONDIAL RECORDING STUDIOS. After checking his files to make sure he had the correct address, Clouseau led the way into the building.

Clouseau and Ponton rode the elevator up

to the recording studio. In the middle of the hallway, a red light was flashing. A sign over the studio door read: DO NOT OPEN DOOR WHEN LIGHT IS FLASHING.

Clouseau waited for the brief instant when the light was between flashes, then noisily yanked open the door and stormed into the room.

Inside the studio, a large orchestra was playing. Next to them, the pop singer, Xania, was singing in a soundproof booth. In a nearby control room, a music producer swayed in time to Xania's singing, which he was recording.

Clouseau began to make his way toward Xania, wading right through the middle of the furiously playing orchestra. As he squeezed between the musicians, he waved his arms to keep his balance. Mesmerized by the riding crop in Clouseau's flailing hand, the musicians began to speed up and slow down their playing. Within seconds, the music dissolved into sonic chaos.

Clouseau didn't notice. He marched straight up to Xania and began to question her, pacing back and forth outside the booth. Her eyes closed tightly, Xania kept right on singing. She couldn't hear a thing.

But the producer could. "Stop! Stop!" he screamed, storming out of the control room. The musicians stopped playing. "Who are you? What are you doing?" he shouted at Clouseau.

Clouseau stopped pacing and stared at him. "I am in the middle of an interrogation!" he exclaimed, offended.

"First," said the producer, "that booth is soundproof; she can't hear a word you're saying. And, in case you haven't noticed, you've just ruined my recording session. Now, get out!" he hollered.

"I am Inspector Clouseau," said Clouseau. As he whipped out his wallet, the police badge flew off, heading toward the producer pin first. Quickly, Ponton intervened and raised the notepad on which he'd been scribbling notes. *Thwack.* The badge got stuck in the pad. Ponton held it up for the producer to see.

"Your name?" Clouseau asked.

"Roland St. Germain," the producer answered.

"And what do you do here?" Clouseau asked.

"I'm the music producer."

"And what is it you produce?" Clouseau asked.

The producer stared at him. "Music."

"Well, Mr. 'Music Producer,'" Clouseau said snidely, "unless you wish to be charged with obstruction of justice, you will allow me to interrogate Mademoiselle Xania."

Just then, Xania stepped out of the booth. "It's all right, Roland," she told the producer.

Clouseau's mouth fell open. Xania was the most beautiful woman he'd ever seen. Gazing into her lovely eyes, Clouseau took her hand and kissed it. Xania smiled at him, pleased.

Suddenly, Clouseau turned to the producer. "Excuse me," he said, "did you say that booth was soundproof?"

"Yes," replied the producer.

To everyone's surprise, Clouseau quickly hurried into the booth and closed the door.

Phhhhbbbbbt! From inside the microphone-filled booth came an amplified, gassy sound that reverberated through the entire studio. Ponton, Xania, the producer, and all of the musicians glanced away, embarrassed.

As Clouseau come out of the booth, blissfully unaware of his musical performance, Ponton decided it was time to get on with their investigation.

"You were nearby when Gluant was killed," he said to Xania.

"Yes," she replied, "I ran out to be with him after the team won."

"Of course you did," Clouseau said, giving her a loving look. "Now, a few hours before the murder, six witnesses saw you repeatedly striking the deceased and screaming . . . What was it, Ponton?"

Ponton checked his notes. "*I'm going to kill you. I'm going to kill you,*" he read.

"I was angry," Xania explained to Clouseau. "I'd caught him with another woman. This was after he'd said he loved me and asked me to marry him. I believed him."

"You poor little angel waif," Clouseau crooned.

"When he cheated on me, I hated him. But I didn't kill him." Xania batted her eyelashes.

"Of course you didn't," Clouseau gushed, staring into her gorgeous face.

"You recently performed in China?" Ponton asked Xania.

Clouseau whirled on him. "Stop browbeating her!" he hissed. "Can't you see she's sexy?"

"Three months ago, in Shanghai," Xania told Ponton.

"And do you know of anyone else who hated Gluant?" asked Clouseau.

"Bizu," said Xania.

Ponton made a note on his pad. "The football star?" he asked.

"I was dating Bizu when I met Gluant," Xania told them. "He thought Gluant was a jerk for stealing me away."

"If you ask me, they were both jerks," the producer said, adding his opinion.

Clouseau glared at him. "You, don't leave town," he said.

"But I'm supposed to fly to Montserrat to record Rene Duchanel," the producer exclaimed. "It's been booked for months."

"You will not leave town," Clouseau repeated. "I may need to ask you a few more questions."

"But I don't know anything."

"About life, about love, you little wet puppy—yes," Clouseau replied. "But about the crime, you may know a lot."

"Do I have to stay in town?" Xania asked. "Next week I have something . . . *vague* to do in New York." She looked away guiltily.

Clouseau smiled at her. "Of course, if you absolutely have to do something vague, feel free to go where you wish," he said. He turned back to the producer. "Don't leave town," he commanded once again.

Clouseau nodded to Ponton, indicating that their work there was done. Then, with one last longing glance at Xania, he headed out the door.

Chapter 6

After leaving the studios, Clouseau and Ponton drove to the headquarters of the French national soccer team to question Bizu. They arrived at a huge, modern-looking building with the Team France logo and the International Championship insignia emblazoned across the front.

Inside, the French team's public-relations representative, a pert young woman named Cherie, greeted them. As she led Clouseau and Ponton down the hall, she explained, " I can't take you to Bizu, but I can take you to Monsieur Vainqueur, the team's assistant coach—well, I guess he's the head coach now," she said.

Clouseau looked at Cherie. "They have a coach for that?" he asked, startled.

"I mean, he's the *main* coach," Cherie told him.

"Oh, I see," said Clouseau.

Turning through a door, they entered a gymnasium filled with workout equipment. A few players kicked soccer balls into practice nets. Other players were doing chin-ups on a high bar.

"Monsieur Gluant hired me," Cherie told the detectives as she led the way through the gym. "We worked very closely. After we hired the trainer away from the Russian military team, we scouted players all over the world."

Seeing the perfect opportunity to surprise-attack Ponton, Clouseau fell back a few steps. As Ponton and Cherie continued to talk, Clouseau crept up behind his partner. Suddenly, he raised his arm, ready for a karate chop.

Wham! Clouseau's arm froze in midair. He looked up and saw that his hand had slammed into an iron chin-up bar.

As Clouseau doubled over in pain, Ponton continued walking, unaware that Clouseau had tried to attack him.

"Were the other women in his life jealous that you worked so closely with Gluant?" Ponton asked Cherie.

"What other women?" Cherie replied. "I mean, the press made a big deal out of the whole Xania thing, but Yves was totally finished with her."

"He told you this?" Clouseau asked, catching up to them. He thrust his smarting hand into his pocket.

"Once. While we were making out," Cherie admitted.

"But we have never made out," Clouseau reminded her.

"I mean, him and me," Cherie said.

"I see." Clouseau frowned, disappointed.

Just then, a muscular man with a pock-marked face strode into the gym. "You wanted to see me?" he asked curtly.

"You are Vainqueur?" Clouseau asked.

"Yes. And who are you?" Vainqueur replied, giving Clouseau an unfriendly look.

"I am Inspector Clouseau," Clouseau pronounced grandly. "Perhaps you have heard of me?"

"No," said Vainqueur.

Clouseau glanced over and saw Ponton making a note. "Don't write that down," he hissed.

"What do you want?" Vainqueur asked them.

"I'm told that Bizu hated Gluant," Clouseau said.

"A lot of people hated Gluant," Vainqueur replied.

"Did you?"

"I spent six years under his thumb, being verbally abused every day. Yes—I was not a fan of Yves Gluant," said Vainqueur.

Clouseau narrow his eyes suspiciously. "Yet now he's dead—and you have his job. Ironic."

Vainqueur shrugged. "Not every death is a tragedy," he replied.

At that moment, they heard footsteps echoing in the corridor outside the gym. Clouseau put his finger to his lips, signaling everyone to be quiet.

"Footsteps," he said, cocking his head to listen. "High heels—rather formal ones for the afternoon—five feet two, brunette. I would say thirty to thirty-five years old."

The footsteps came up to the door. The door opened, and a short, stocky man in sweatpants entered the gym.

Clouseau looked around. "Is anyone with you?" he asked.

"No," said the man.

"You have high heels in that bag?" Clouseau asked, eyeing the training bag on the man's shoulder.

"No."

"Not even a small pair of pumps?"

"No."

"Who are you?" Clouseau asked.

"I'm Yuri, the trainer," the man replied.

"And what is it you do here?" asked Clouseau.

"I'm the trainer," Yuri repeated.

Again, Clouseau narrowed his eyes. A likely story, he thought. "You are Yuri, the trainer who trains," he said disbelievingly. "DO NOT LEAVE EUROPE!"

"But I have to go to Asia," Yuri told him.

"Asia is okay," Clouseau said. "BUT DO NOT LEAVE ASIA OR EUROPE!"

"We have one game in Brazil," Yuri added.

"All right," Clouseau agreed wearily. "DO NOT LEAVE ASIA, EUROPE, OR THE AMERICAS!"

As Yuri left the gym, Clouseau turned back to Vainqueur. "And what about Bizu?" he asked. "Did he hate Gluant?"

"Yes," Vainqueur answered.

"And where is he now?"

"Outside. On the practice field."

"Well," said Clouseau, "we shall see about Mr. Bizu." He kicked a soccer ball, to show what would happen to Bizu if he didn't cooperate.

Whack! The ball bounced up and smacked Clouseau in the head.

Chapter 8

In the interrogation room at the Palais de la Justice, Bizu sat in a hard wooden seat, squinting under the bright, hot lights. Inspector Clouseau paced back and forth in front of him, scowling.

"You are the soccer player known as Bizu?" Clouseau demanded.

"Yes," Bizu replied, giving the inspector a surly look.

"You were acquainted with Yves Gluant?" Clouseau asked.

"I hope he burns in hell," Bizu snarled.

"Is it true that you harbored a dislike for him?" Clouseau asked.

"I'm glad he's pushing up daisies," Bizu replied angrily.

"He is not pushing up daisies," Clouseau shouted. "He is dead!"

Bizu sneered at him. "It's an idiom," he explained.

"You, sir, are the idiom!" Clouseau yelled. He put his face right up to Bizu's. "Unless you want to spend the rest of your life in prison, you will answer the next question. Did you kill him?"

Bizu didn't flinch. "I would have loved to have killed him," he said hotly. "But some lucky person beat me to it!"

"You disgust me," Clouseau spat. "I'll be right back." Abruptly, he turned and walked out the door.

A moment later, Clouseau returned, smiling. "Cigarette?" he asked. He held a pack out toward Bizu.

"No, thanks," Bizu said.

"Good for you," said Clouseau. He gave the soccer player a friendly look. "Bizu, I know you didn't do it."

"Good," Bizu said, surprised by Clouseau's sudden change of attitude.

"Someone else did, and they are trying to set you up," Clouseau told him.

"You'll help me?" Bizu asked.

"Of course," Clouseau replied. "Do you have any idea who might have done it?"

"You want my guess?" said Bizu. "His partner in those stupid restaurants—Larocque."

"Raymond Larocque, who owns the casinos?" Clouseau asked.

"Gluant would steal money from the restaurants and use it to gamble," Bizu said. "He used to brag about what a sucker Larocque was. My guess is that Larocque got fed up and had him killed. And if ever someone deserved to die, it was that stinking pig!"

Clouseau nodded. "I like you, Bizu," he said. "I'll be right back." He hurried out the door.

Out in the hallway, Clouseau picked up a black electrical box with two wires dangling from it and a small plunger in the center. Ponton saw him and walked over.

"What are you doing?" he asked.

"I'm giving him the good-cop, bad-cop routine," Clouseau explained.

Ponton frowned. "Usually, two *different* cops do that," he said.

"Yes. But with today's budget cuts . . ." Clouseau shrugged and walked back into the interrogation room as Ponton stared after him, speechless.

"Well, Bizu," Clouseau snarled, returning to his bad-cop routine. "You may have heard what we do to people who don't cooperate." He placed the ominous-looking electrical box on the table. "We hook them up to the 'box.'"

Bizu's eyes widened at the sight of the strange contraption. "What is the box?" he asked fearfully.

"These two electrodes," Clouseau said, holding up two wires, "each one down your pants."

"How?" Bizu asked.

"Idiot," Clouseau scoffed. "Like this. One goes here . . . and one goes here." Taking the electrodes, he stuck them down his own pants.

"By the way," he added, "don't touch the plunger—*ahhhhhhhhhhhhhh!*"

Clouseau's scream echoed down the hall of the police station. A moment later, he emerged from the interrogation room with smoke pouring from his pants.

In the hall he met Ponton. Clouseau explained that he was done with his questions and suggested they call it a day.

"Bizu might be a soccer great," Clouseau said as they walked toward his car a short while later. "But he cannot stand up to an interrogation by Inspector Clouseau. I have definitely come to a conclusion about Mr. Bizu."

When they reached the car, Ponton got behind the wheel. Clouseau climbed into the passenger's seat. Smoke was still streaming from his pants.

"So, what do you think?" asked Ponton as he maneuvered the car out into the street.

"Bizu is innocent," Clouseau declared, staring out the window at a cyclist in racing gear who had pulled up alongside the car.

"How can you say that?" Ponton exclaimed. Frustrated, he pressed down on the gas pedal. The car pulled ahead of the cyclist. "Gluant suspended Bizu. He stole his girlfriend. And then, in front of the whole world, he took Bizu out of the semifinals. If it were me, I would have killed him then and there. And that's exactly what Bizu did!"

"Ponton, Ponton," Clouseau said calmly, "a crime is like a jigsaw puzzle. You have to have the jig, and you have to have the saw."

As they pulled up to Clouseau's apartment, Clouseau threw open his door, then turned back to Ponton. "All you have is the jig," he added. "You have no saw. Where is your saw?"

Wham! The furiously pedaling cyclist smacked into the open car door and went flying into the air.

"Ahhhhhhh!" the cyclist screamed.

Clouseau didn't notice. "What?" he asked when he saw the alarmed look on Ponton's face.

Ponton suddenly felt exhausted. "Nothing," he replied. Clouseau closed the door and Ponton drove off.

Just then, Clouseau noticed the bicycle lying in the street. He looked around for its rider, but saw no one.

"Strange," Clouseau murmured. He started toward his apartment.

In the middle of the intersection, the bicyclist picked himself up from where he'd landed and began to march angrily toward Clouseau.

Wham! The bicyclist was suddenly knocked down by a large, fast-moving object. It was the wooden globe from Clouseau's office! The globe flatted the cyclist, then rolled on down the street.

Clouseau paused and looked around suspiciously, sensing something amiss. But he saw nothing out of the ordinary. Shrugging, he turned and walked into his apartment.

Meanwhile, in Inspector Dreyfus's office, Dreyfus and Agent Renard were watching a newscast of the Pink Panther–diamond press conference. Dreyfus frowned, worried, as Clouseau's face filled the TV screen.

"Killer, I will find you," Clouseau declared on the television, "because I am a servant of the nation . . . because justice is justice . . . and because France is France!" As he finished, the camera pulled back to show the police officers in the room cheering wildly.

"With reporters already calling him the Pink Panther detective," the television news anchor declared, "it seems a new hero has arrived, bringing hope to a nation still mourning the loss of a legend. And that's the news."

Dreyfus shut off the television.

"Pink Panther detective!" he snarled in disgust. "That's absurd! He's done absolutely nothing, and already they're playing him as a hero."

"He gave them a good sound bite," Renard pointed out.

Dreyfus began to pace the room. He knew Renard was right and it worried him. If anything got in the way of his receiving the Medal of Honor . . .

"We have to be careful," he told Renard finally. "He may not be as stupid as we think."

Chapter 9

When Clouseau arrived at his apartment, he noticed something strange. The front door was slightly ajar.

Instantly, Clouseau was on his guard. He pulled out his revolver and checked the chamber. There were six bullets. Silently, Clouseau snapped the chamber shut and raised the weapon to his shoulder.

But the chamber hadn't closed all the way. As he lifted the gun, all of the bullets spilled out onto the floor. Clouseau didn't notice.

Balancing on a rail at the side of the door, Clouseau ran his fingers along the doorsill, checking for booby traps. Then he ran his fingers across the top of the door to see if it had been bugged.

Slam! The door suddenly closed—right on Clouseau's finger. He fell from the railing and dangled by his fingertips, squirming in pain. With his other hand, he reached for the doorbell, but it was too far away. He fired his gun at the doorknob. But the gun was empty.

Frantically, Clouseau kicked the door.

Suddenly, the door opened. Nicole stood in the doorway. She stared in astonishment, as Clouseau collapsed to the floor.

Gently, Nicole helped Clouseau to a chair. She found a container of salve in a cabinet, and rubbed some onto Clouseau's throbbing finger.

"Feeling any better?" she asked after a bit.

"Yes, thank you," Clouseau replied, not entirely truthfully.

"I hope you don't mind," Nicole said. "I let myself in with the spare key." She'd dropped by his apartment to deliver his clothes. "And look. . . ." Nicole added. Opening a bag, she pulled out two pairs of pants. "I got the pants back from the tailor, plus a spare."

She noticed a pained look on Clouseau's face as he eyed his swollen finger. "Would you like some water?" she asked him.

"Please," Clouseau said.

Nicole opened the refrigerator and grabbed a bottle of water. Spying a hard-boiled egg in a bowl, she held it up. "Do you mind if I have this?" she asked Clouseau. "I haven't eaten."

"Certainly," he replied.

Nicole raised the egg to her lips. But before she could take a bite, the slippery egg suddenly slid from her fingers and lodged in the back of her throat. Nicole began to choke. She wheeled around the kitchen, trying to catch her breath.

Clouseau didn't notice. With his back turned to Nicole, he mused, "Everything I have learned in my lifetime of investigation is coming into play."

Nicole flailed her arms. Her face turned red.

"Things are appearing in my mind that I did not even remember I knew," Clouseau went on. When Nicole didn't respond, he looked around. "Oh, *mon Dieu*!" he cried, noticing her distress at last. "The Heimlich! The Heimlich!"

Running to Nicole, he grasped her from behind and began to lift her off the ground, trying to dislodge the egg.

Just then, there was a knock at the door. The door opened, and Ponton stood on the threshold. His eyes widened when he saw Clouseau and Nicole.

"Don't worry, Ponton," Clouseau said with a gasp. "We're almost there."

Pop! The egg shot out of Nicole's mouth and flew through the open window.

"Ahhhhh!" Nicole sighed, gasping for air.

"Feel better?" Clouseau asked her.

"Yes, thank you," Nicole said with relief. "Where did you learn that?"

"I used to practice on mannequins," Clouseau told her. "And frankly, you looked like you needed it. Now . . ." He turned to Ponton in a businesslike manner. "What do you have for me, Ponton?"

Ponton closed his mouth, which had been

gaping open, and replied, "It seems you were right about Bizu. He was just found dead in the training-facility locker room. Shot in the head."

"Was it fatal?" Clouseau asked.

"Yes," said Ponton.

"How fatal?"

Ponton frowned. "Completely."

Clouseau began to pace around the room. "I want to talk to him now!" he exclaimed.

"He's dead," Ponton reminded him.

"Ah." Clouseau nodded, as if Ponton had made a good point. "Were there any witnesses?" he asked.

"Only one," said Ponton.

It was dark by the time they reached the Team France headquarters. They found Cherie, the young PR representative, in the locker room. She was the one who had discovered Bizu's body.

"Please tell me what you saw," Clouseau said.

"Well, I didn't see anything," Cherie replied, her voice shaking. "I was passing by the locker room. It was late, past time that anyone should be there. I heard movement on the other side of the locker-room door. I heard Bizu say, 'Oh, it's you.' And then there was gunfire."

Clouseau nodded and pulled Ponton aside.

"Go to your databases," he instructed him. "I want to interrogate every person in Paris with the name 'You.'"

He glanced down at the locker-room floor, where a chalk outline showed the position of Bizu's fallen body. "Ponton," he added, lowering his voice, "don't you find it a bit of a coincidence that the body fell perfectly within the chalk outline on the floor?"

"I think they drew the chalk outline later," Ponton replied patiently.

"Ah," said Clouseau. "We are facing a mastermind. Ponton, we are going to the casino to interview this man, Raymond Larocque. Where is his casino?"

Ponton smiled. "In the most beautiful city in the world," he replied.

Chapter 10

Late that night, Clouseau and Ponton arrived in Rome. As they pulled up to Larocque's grand casino, they saw that the parking lot was filled with the limousines and sports cars of Europe's wealthiest citizens.

"You really believe this casino owner killed Gluant?" Ponton asked Clouseau doubtfully, as they exited Clouseau's tiny car.

"I keep my mind open like a steel trap," said Clouseau.

He handed the car keys to a parking attendant. "Keep it close by . . . if you know what's good for you." Clouseau carefully flashed his police badge at the attendant. This time the badge stayed in his wallet.

The attendant nodded. As Clouseau and Ponton entered the casino, the attendant parked Clouseau's little car next to a row of Rolls-Royces. It looked like a Chihuahua in a row of Great Danes.

Inside the casino, elegant people in expensive gowns and silk suits were standing around tables, playing high-stakes games of blackjack and baccarat. Beautiful waitresses moved through the crowd carrying drinks.

As the detectives cased the room, Clouseau paused by the roulette table.

"Ponton, go find out where Larocque's office is," he instructed. "I will wait here."

Ponton looked surprised. "You are going to gamble?" he asked Clouseau.

"Of course not," Clouseau scoffed. "They are all fools. Don't they know the odds are stacked against them?" He eyed the roulette table. "You should only gamble what you can afford to lose," he added sagely.

When Ponton had gone, Clouseau wandered

over to the roulette table and placed a single coin on a black number. The croupier spun the wheel, and the ball landed on red. The croupier swept up his coin. Clouseau stared in pained silence at the spot where it had been.

Just then, he overheard someone proclaim, "IT IS NICE WEATHER WE'RE HAVING. I HOPE THE WEATHER CONTINUES."

Clouseau looked over and saw a handsome, well-dressed man talking to a plump man standing next to him.

"IF THE WEATHER STAYS THIS MILD, WE'RE ALL IN FOR A TREAT!" the handsome man continued at full volume.

Clouseau leaned in close to his ear. "I am in law enforcement, too," he murmured.

The man frowned. "Am I that obvious?" he whispered back.

"No," Clouseau told him. "It's just that I have an ear for such things."

Just then, a waitress walked up to them. "Here is your Mojito," she said holding a drink out to the good-looking man.

"Flame it," the man instructed.

The waitress lit the drink on fire. It flamed briefly. The man took a sip from the straw.

Clouseau raised his eyebrows. "Impressive," he said. "I will remember that." Then he lowered his voice and whispered, "I am Inspector Jacques Clouseau. I am here on a very important case."

"I am Nigel Boswell," the man whispered back. "Agent Double-Oh-Six. You know what that means?"

"Of course I do," Clouseau replied. "One short of the big time."

"I am on a very important case," Boswell explained. "So you will understand what I mean, Inspector, when I tell you that I am not here."

"Of course I understand. You are not here," Clouseau repeated.

"I am supposed to be in Switzerland," Boswell told him.

"You are not here, you are in Switzerland," said Clouseau.

"I am following a very important Colombian

drug lord," Boswell went on. "No one must know I am here."

"I have just slipped my cell phone number into your pocket. YES, THE WEATHER IS LOVELY THIS YEAR." Clouseau shouted as someone passed close to them. "Call me if you need anything," he whispered to Boswell. Then he slipped away.

Clouseau met up with Ponton at the casino's security desk.

"Please inform Monsieur Larocque that Inspector Clouseau of the Police Nationale wishes to have a word with him," Ponton told the supervisor.

The supervisor nodded and picked up the phone.

Moments later, Clouseau and Ponton were ushered into a luxurious penthouse apartment. Antique Chinese vases decorated the tables, and silk rugs covered the floor. Exotic fish darted through a huge aquarium. A thin, elegant man in his late fifties stood in the center of the room, leaning on an ornate walking stick.

But Clouseau barely glanced at him. He was far more interested in the oil paintings on the walls.

"Monet!" he cried, recognizing the work of the famous French artist. He turned to the painting next to it. "Renoir!" he declared. The next painting was a famous work by the artist Gauguin. "Gwen-gwan!" Clouseau happily garbled the name.

The elegant man stepped forward. "Very impressive, Inspector Clouseau. How can I help you?"

"You're Raymond Larocque?" Clouseau asked, finally noticing him.

"Yes."

"I am investigating the death of Yves Gluant," Clouseau informed him.

"Ah, Yves . . . Fascinating man," said Larocque. He paused, then asked, "Would you like a drink? Huang . . ." Larocque turned to his bodyguard. "Pour the gentlemen a drink, would you?"

A huge, menacing-looking Chinese man emerged from the shadows. "Drink?" he inquired, with a threatening glare.

Ponton looked at Clouseau, who shook his head sternly.

"Not while on duty," Ponton told Huang.

Huang looked at Clouseau. "You?"

"Grenadine with a little Pernod," Clouseau replied.

"Oh, I haven't made one of those in years!" Huang exclaimed gaily. He bustled over to the bar to make the drink.

"Tell me, monsieur," Clouseau said, turning back to Larocque, "do you happen to know what Gluant paid for his ring?"

"He inherited it. It cost him nothing," Larocque replied.

"It cost him his *life*!" Clouseau retorted. He took a step closer to Larocque. "I would like to take a closer look at your bawls," he said.

"What?" Larocque asked. He wasn't sure he had heard correctly.

"I would like to take a look at your big, brass

bawls!" Clouseau exclaimed. He walked over to a side table and carefully inspected the brass bowl sitting atop it. "Hmmm. Eighteenth century. Han dynasty," Clouseau declared.

"You have an eye for antiques, Inspector," Larocque told him. "Some here are real, some are copies. I'm sure you can tell which ones are which."

Clouseau moved over to examine two antique Chinese vases. A sign next to them read: BEWARE, EASY TO GET HAND CAUGHT IN VASES.

"One must always handle a ceramic from the inside. The oil from the hands can change the patina," Clouseau explained, plunging his hand into the vase. He held it up to the light. "Hmmm. Pure alabaster."

He started to put the vase back down. But his hand was stuck.

"That's odd," he said, furrowing his brow. "All I did was . . ." Reaching over, he stuck his hand in the other vase. Now both of his hands were caught.

As Clouseau wriggled around, trying to get

his hands free, Ponton turned to Larocque. "You took out a life insurance policy on Gluant?" he asked.

"The insurance company won't pay until the murderer is caught," Larocque replied. "And if it turns out to be me, they won't pay at all! Look, when the killer is found, I'll get some insurance money, and I can try to sue the estate for the ring. Believe me, I want the guy caught as much as anyone."

"But you stood to *gain* from Gluant's death, didn't you?" Clouseau interrupted, giving up his struggle. He casually leaned against the aquarium, trying to look like someone who didn't have an antique Chinese vase stuck on each hand.

"Gain? What would I gain?" Larocque asked.

"Gluant's share of the restaurants," Clouseau replied. His elbow grazed the top of the water in the fish tank. The fish went into a piranha-like feeding frenzy, tearing the elbow of his jacket to shreds. Clouseau didn't notice.

"The restaurants were a disaster!" Larocque exclaimed. "Gluant was siphoning money out faster than it came in. My only consolation was he'd lose the money gambling in my casino. But after a while, his losses were getting so ridiculous that he promised me his diamond ring as collateral."

"But *you* had words with Gluant the night before he was killed, didn't you?" Clouseau suddenly cried, whipping around to point at Huang. The vase popped off his hand and flew straight at Huang's head.

Huang ducked. Ponton caught the vase and set it down.

"No," Huang replied.

"You didn't threaten to break his arms and legs and crush them into powder?" cried Clouseau.

"No," said Huang.

"Well, then, perhaps I misunderstood," Clouseau said. As the others watched, he went back to struggling with the remaining vase. He twisted and tugged, but the hand was stuck fast.

At last, he turned to Larocque. "Excuse me, is this vase of great value?" he asked.

"It is a worthless imitation," Larocque assured him.

"Ah, good," said Clouseau. Raising his hand, he struck the vase against an end table. The vase shattered into a thousand pieces. And so did the table.

Everyone stared at the destroyed table, aghast.

"But that desk was priceless," Larocque said.

Just then, Clouseau's cell phone rang. He fumbled around in his coat pocket until he found it.

"It is I," he said, when he heard the voice on the other end. "Well, yes . . . I can meet you. In the restaurant? Yes, right away." Hanging up the phone, he turned to the other men. "Gentlemen, I hope you will excuse me for a moment. Something very important has come up."

And without further explanation, Clouseau hurried out.

Returning to the main floor, Clouseau ran

through the casino, which now was filled with masked men.

Clouseau stopped one of the men just as he was putting on a gas mask.

"Excuse me," he said, "can you tell me where the restaurant is?"

The man pointed to a large window overlooking the casino. "It is up there," he replied in a heavy Italian accent.

Clouseau raced up the stairs. He found Nigel Boswell, apparently waiting for him in the empty, darkened restaurant.

"Clouseau!" Boswell whispered. "I need your help. Take a look behind you."

Clouseau looked through the plate-glass window at the way he'd just come. Below, on the casino floor, bandits in gas masks were weaving through the crowd of gamblers, dropping cans of noxious gas. As the crowd started to choke, the bandits scooped up money from the gambling tables.

"Oh, my God. Thieves," said Clouseau.

"They are the Gas-Mask Bandits," Boswell

told him. "All Europe is looking for them."

"I am ready," Clouseau declared, striking a karate stance. "How can I help?"

"All I need is your coat," Boswell told him.

Clouseau handed it over. "Why?" he asked.

"I am not supposed to be here, remember?" Boswell said. "I can't blow my cover, but I can't let the Gas-Mask Bandits escape!"

Opening his briefcase, Boswell pulled out a gas mask and placed it over his head. Then he took out a high–tech glass cutter and cut a neat circle in the window, silently removing the cutout piece with a suction cup. Now there was a hole in the glass large enough for a man to fit through.

Boswell inserted a grappling hook attached to a steel cord through the opening in the glass. The hook caught on the other side of the room. Wearing Clouseau's coat, Boswell slid down the cord and dropped a small canister into the casino. As soon as the canister hit the floor and broke open, the air began to clear.

Boswell pulled out a sleeping-dart gun. One

When Chief Inspector Dreyfus calls Clouseau to Paris, Clouseau is quick to respond. This is a big honor!

At a press conference Dreyfus introduces Clouseau as the inspector on the Gluant murder case. But Dreyfus has other plans. . . . He secretly wants to solve the case himself.

Gilbert Ponton is assigned to work with Clouseau on
the soccer coach's murder case, and will help him
find the missing Pink Panther diamond.

One suspect is very beautiful. Xania, Gluant's
girlfriend, is a pop singer. She tells Clouseau that
she is innocent . . . and he believes her.

Another suspect, Monsieur Larocque, owns a casino. Will the clue be red or black?

Ponton questions Monsieur Larocque, while
Clouseau inspects some priceless vases in his
apartment.

Dreyfus is suspicious of Clouseau. But his snooping
around gets him a black eye!

When Xania heads for New York City, Clouseau and Ponton follow her to the Big Apple, in a New York minute.

Clouseau meets Xania for a date. . . . Will he get more information?

On his hot date with Xania, Clouseau tries to
look cool—even when his drink catches fire!

Clouseau has a plan to catch the murderer at the President's Ball, with Ponton and Dreyfus's secretary, Nicole, there to help.

Great disguises! Clouseau and Ponton make their way around the ballroom without being seen.

The prestigious Medal of Honor ceremony, where Clouseau is honored for solving the famous Pink Panther case.

Inspector Clouseau is now the most famous inspector in France. The murderer is captured, and the Pink Panther diamond is found! Bravo, Clouseau!

by one, he shot down the bandits, then slid back across the steel cord. He was back in the restaurant in less than a minute.

Quickly he swapped coats with Clouseau, then handed him the gas mask and the grappling hook.

"Inspector," Boswell said, saluting Clouseau. A second later, he zipped through a panel in the ceiling and was gone.

Just then, the doors of the restaurant burst open. Security guards and casino workers rushed into the room. They saw Clouseau standing next to the plate-glass window, holding the gas mask and grappling hook.

"My God, man, that was fantastic!" cried the security chief.

Clouseau smiled for the cameras as photographers swarmed around him, snapping his picture.

Chapter 11

The next morning, photos of Clouseau were on the front page of every newspaper in Europe. Overnight he'd become known as the hero who had single-handedly stopped the Gas-Mask Bandits.

But Clouseau didn't have time to revel in his "victory." When he arrived at work that morning, Ponton was waiting for him.

"Inspector, we have rounded up all the people in Paris with the name 'You,'" he told Clouseau.

The Inspector smiled. "Now we are getting somewhere."

Ponton led Clouseau to the interrogation

room, where an elderly Chinese woman named Mrs. Yu was sitting under harsh, bright lights. Clouseau silently circled around the woman.

"Where were you on the night that Gluant was murdered?" he demanded.

Mrs. Yu let loose a long tirade in Chinese.

Clouseau blinked. "You may go," he said.

Another policeman escorted her out. Ponton asked Clouseau in disbelief, "You speak Chinese?"

"Of course I speak Chinese! You think I don't speak Chinese?" Clouseau snapped. "How can you think I don't speak Chinese? Oh, so now Inspector Clouseau does not speak Chinese. Then what are we doing here?" He glowered at Ponton, going on to mutter, "Does not speak Chinese. Oh, that is funny. How could I not speak Chinese?"

While Clouseau and Ponton were busy in the interrogation room, Dreyfus decided to search Clouseau's office. All morning long he had been hounded by reporters wanting to know whether the Gas-Mask Bandits were somehow connected to Gluant's murder. Dreyfus was furious that Clouseau was getting so much attention. And now he was determined to find out just how much Clouseau really knew about the case.

Dreyfus sat down at Clouseau's desk and began to poke through the drawers. Finding Clouseau's address book, he flipped through the pages. It was filled with the fan-mail addresses of a number of sexy pop stars. He opened a side drawer. In it sat a year's supply of mustache dye, but nothing more.

Spying Clouseau's briefcase on the desk, he popped it open and began to sift through the contents. Just then, he heard Clouseau's voice in the hallway.

"*Bonjour,* Nicole," Clouseau said. "Can you meet me in my office in a few minutes?"

Dreyfus looked around for a place to hide, then darted behind the curtains.

A moment later, Clouseau entered the room. He paused, sensing that something was wrong.

The things on his desk were not exactly where he had left them.

Clouseau stooped beneath the desk and picked up a single hair—the very hair he had placed in his top drawer on his first day in the office. Now he knew someone had been looking through his desk.

Clouseau quickly scanned the room. His eyes lit on the curtains. Two polished leather loafers were sticking out from beneath them.

"Nicole," Clouseau called, "could I see you now?"

"Yes, Inspector?" Nicole entered the room, then stopped. Clouseau was creeping toward the windows, grasping a wooden chair.

"Ah, Nicole. THE WEATHER IS SO PLEASANT," Clouseau shouted. "I WAS WONDERING IF YOU THINK THE WEATHER IS GOING TO STAY THIS MILD."

"I certainly hope so. . . ." Nicole began.

"BUT DO YOU THINK THE WEATHER IS GOING TO CHANGE?" Clouseau asked, signaling Nicole to stand back from the window.

"Let's keep our fingers crossed that it stays this mild," Nicole replied.

Wham! Clouseau smashed the chair against the curtains. With a groan, Dreyfus fell to the floor.

"How diabolical!" Clouseau exclaimed. "Thinking you can fool me with that Inspector Dreyfus flesh mask? Now, let's see who you really are!"

With an aggressive pull, Clouseau tried to rip off what he thought was a mask. The fact that the mask wouldn't budge made him yank harder.

Clearly, this was no mask, but Dreyfus!

Clouseau would not give up. "Ah, you've really got it stuck on there tightly, don't you?!" Clouseau dragged Dreyfus around the office by his face.

A short time later, Clouseau came to check on Dreyfus. Dreyfus was sitting on his desk, holding an ice pack to his swelling check. His eye was already turning purple.

"Are you feeling better?" Clouseau asked,

hurrying over to him. "I am so sorry, Inspector."

"Let's just forget about it," Dreyfus said, leaping up and quickly moving his desk between him and the hazardous Clouseau.

"Well, then, I just thought I would stop by to let you know where we are on the case," Clouseau said. He sat down on a corner of the desk.

"Good," replied Dreyfus, inching back in his chair. "I'll just stay here."

"Ah, I see you have one of these collapsible pointers," Clouseau said, picking it up from the desk to admire it. "Very useful. It's so degrading to have to use your finger or a long wooden stick. It's like you are an oaf. But one of these, you just snap it open. . . ." Clouseau snapped opened the pointer, whacking Dreyfus in the face. "And you are ready to go."

"The case, Inspector," Dreyfus said, mustering every ounce of patience he had.

"Ah, yes. The case is going quite well," said Clouseau. "You see, Inspector, the crime has three components: the soccer stadium; the people immediately surrounding Gluant; and a small circle of friends. And from that I have made up a list of suspects."

"How many suspects does that give you?" Gluant asked.

"Twenty-seven thousand six hundred and eighty-three," said Clouseau.

Dreyfus stared at him. "Twenty-seven thousand, six hundred and eighty-three," he repeated.

"Yes."

Dreyfus could barely hide his delight. Clouseau was every bit as idiotic as he'd hoped. "It sounds like it's only a matter of time," he told Clouseau. "Have you eliminated any of the suspects?"

"Yes, one," said Clouseau.

"One. And who is that?"

"Gluant."

"Gluant is the victim," Dreyfus pointed out.

"Excellent, Inspector. We think alike," said Clouseau. He got up to leave. "As you were at the game, Inspector," he added, heading toward the door, "I would love to have you think back. Try to remember if you saw anything suspicious, anyone running around with a poison-dart gun. . . ."

"I will," Dreyfus assured him.

"I assure you, Inspector, I soon will have your murderer cornered like a kangaroo . . . without a . . . car," Clouseau said.

"Very well put," Dreyfus said indulgently.

"Ah." Clouseau brightened. "I see you enjoy wordplay. I, too, take delight in a little verbal jousting."

"You are a raconteur," said Dreyfus.

"Yes," Clouseau agreed. He had no idea what Dreyfus was talking about. "A rac . . . rac . . . yes. Whatever." Just then he noticed the metal fili-gree, which had been replaced on the door frame. "I see you have repaired the beautiful molding around the door. Today's French craftsmen are every bit as good as those of the eighteenth century. . . ."

As he spoke, Clouseau fiddled with the fili-gree. Once again, it came off in his hands. "I'll put it here. It looks good anywhere," he said, leaning it against a wall. Then he hurried out the door.

Dreyfus stared after him, fuming. Just then the corner of the desk where Clouseau had been sitting collapsed, and everything on it spilled to the floor.

"Maintenance!" Dreyfus shouted furiously.

Just a few more days, Dreyfus promised himself, and then he would have the Medal of Honor, and Clouseau would return to a life of obscurity—which he deserved.

Chapter 12

That afternoon, a committee met in the French presidential offices to discuss the nominees for the Medal of Honor.

"Only two names have been put forward this year," the president explained, addressing the room full of dignitaries, "but both exemplify the highest standards of heroic service. The two nominees are Charles Dreyfus, chief Inspector of the national police, who you may recall broke the Marseille cocaine cartel earlier in the year. . . ."

The dignitaries applauded politely. Dreyfus flashed a practiced smile. He had covered the bruises on his face with makeup. Only a faint mark remained on his cheek.

"And Sister Marie-Hugette of the Ursuline Sisters," the president continued, "whose selfless concerns for our nation's orphans is an inspiration to us all."

Again the room applauded. In a show of goodwill, Dreyfus smiled warmly at the plump nun. Then he turned to agent Renard, who was standing along the wall with the other deputies, and rolled his eyes. Renard gave him a thumbs-up. There was no way Dreyfus could lose to the nun. They were sure of that.

Just then, Monsieur Clochard, the minister of justice, raised his hand. "Excuse me, Monsieur President," he said. "I would like to add one more name for the committee's consideration."

Everyone turned to him, surprised.

"Inspector Jacques Clouseau," Clochard said to the crowd, "the man who came here from a small village to investigate the murder of Yves Gluant, who just last night captured the notorious Gas-Mask Bandits."

"Interesting idea," the president said thoughtfully, "an average Frenchman . . ."

"Exactly," Clochard agreed. Around the room, heads began to nod.

"But his principal task is to find Gluant's killer," Dreyfus interjected, his eyes burning with anger, "which he hasn't done. So, in point of fact, Clouseau has failed at his most important assignment."

"Of course, he would only be considered if he finds the killer," Clochard agreed.

"But if he does, it might give the young voters new faith in our administration," said the president. "Excellent idea! All in favor?"

To Dreyfus's horror, every single hand in the room went up.

Dreyfus stormed back to the Palais de la Justice and called Ponton into his office.

"How is it that I was not informed of Clouseau going to that casino?" the chief inspector shouted, his face red with anger.

"It was the middle of the night," Ponton replied.

"Don't give me excuses!" Dreyfus bellowed. "I want a report on Clouseau's whereabouts every hour, twenty-four hours a day! Miss a call and I'll have you kicked off the force. Do you understand?"

"Yes, sir," said Ponton.

By the time Ponton left Dreyfus's office, it was late afternoon. Ponton found Clouseau walking home to his apartment along the Seine.

"Ah, Ponton," Clouseau said when the young detective caught up with him. "Let's call it a day. I am tired."

"I just wanted to see where you are with the investigation," Ponton said.

"Good idea, Ponton. To let the subconscious mind work on the case while we sleep. Now then, what are the facts?" Clouseau said.

"Yves Gluant was found at the International Championship Semifinal with a poison dart in his neck. . . ." Ponton began.

"The crime!" shouted Clouseau.

"Bizu wanted to kill him, but is now himself

90

dead. . . ." Ponton said.

"A complication!" Clouseau exclaimed.

"Gluant was siphoning off money from Larocque. . . ."

"A motive!" Clouseau declared.

"And right next to the body was the singer Xania," Ponton finished.

"I want her!" Clouseau cried.

"What?" Ponton stared at him.

"Nothing," Clouseau said quickly. "Now then, what is the inescapable conclusion?"

"That the singer Xania killed Yves Gluant," Ponton replied.

Clouseau shook his head. "Oh, you poor, sick little sidekick."

"Xania is the killer!" Ponton exclaimed, no longer able to hold back his emotions. "I'm trying to help you. I've grown fond of you. You don't want to see it, because you're in love with her!"

"Xania is not the killer," Clouseau said patiently, "but I suspect that she knows more than she is telling me. Where is she now?"

"She left suddenly for New York," Ponton told him.

Clouseau's eyes narrowed. "And where is this New York?"

"In America," Ponton explained patiently.

"Well, Ponton, we are going to follow her to New York and find out what she is up to," Clouseau said. Without warning, he raised his hand to strike Ponton.

Ponton punched him first.

"Now," when Clouseau recovered, he went on, "if I am going to America, I will have to learn to speak with a flawless American accent, so as not to arouse suspicion. Find me the greatest accent coach," he told Ponton.

Ponton frowned, but walked off to do as he was asked. Still, he couldn't help thinking that Clouseau was making a huge mistake.

Chapter 13

The first thing Clouseau and Ponton did when they arrived in New York was to visit a hamburger stand. Clouseau had been working hard on his American accent, and he was eager to try it out.

"Hello," he said to the vendor, trying to sound like a real New Yorker. "I would like to buy a hamburger." He gave the vendor a huge, American-style grin.

The vendor stared at him. Clouseau's American accent was just as ridiculous as his French one.

"With mustard and ketchup, please, and thank you," Clouseau added, feeling very satisfied with himself.

When he had finished his hamburger, Clouseau and Ponton went to their hotel. Clouseau had insisted that he should do all the talking, since he had now mastered the American way of speaking.

"I would like to get a hotel room," Clouseau told the front-desk clerk.

The clerk, who was French, smirked. "Certainly, sir," he said. Turning to another clerk, he murmured in French, "Stupid American." The other clerk snickered, thinking Clouseau hadn't understood.

Clouseau gave the clerk a huge American smile. "May I see your pen?" he asked.

Annoyed, the clerk took the pen from his shirt pocket and handed it over. Clouseau looked at it a moment, then handed it back. "Have a good one!" he said, still speaking in an exaggerated American accent.

As Clouseau walked away, the clerk sneered at his back, unaware of the huge ink stain that was spreading across his shirt.

Early the next morning, Clouseau and

Ponton stationed themselves outside the Waldorf Astoria—the hotel where Xania was staying.

"I got her hotel phone records," Ponton told Clouseau. "She made two phone calls to a notorious black-market diamond-cutter."

"There she is," said Clouseau, spying Xania walk out the door. "Perhaps she will take us to him."

Clouseau and Ponton trailed Xania down the block. When she glanced back over her shoulder, they held newspapers up in front of their faces to disguise themselves.

They followed the singer downtown to an unmarked building in a run-down block of old warehouses. Xania looked both ways, then entered the building.

"Newspapers!" cried Clouseau. Still hiding behind his paper, he didn't see a set of steps leading down to a subway station.

"Ahhh!" he cried as he tumbled down the stairs.

By the time Clouseau and Ponton got into

the building, Xania had disappeared into an elevator. Clouseau and Ponton watched the numbers move as the elevator traveled up. It stopped on the twelfth floor.

"I smell something fishy," Clouseau remarked.

Just then, the doors of another elevator opened. Three men in black suits and dark sunglasses stepped out. They strode menacingly toward Clouseau and Ponton.

"May I help you?" one man said.

"We are looking for a black-market diamond-cutter," Clouseau said in his American accent.

"I don't know of any diamond-cutter," the man said.

"Oh, really?" said Clouseau. *Wham!* He karate-chopped the man. At once a fight broke out. Ponton stepped in, flipping one man over his shoulder and punching the other two. A moment later, the three men lay in a heap on the ground.

The elevator arrived, and Ponton and Clouseau got in. They pushed the button for the twelfth floor. But when they had only gone as far as the sixth floor, the elevator stopped.

"An unscheduled stop," Clouseau said knowingly. The detectives struck several karate poses.

When the doors opened, two Chinese men got in. Clouseau sized them up. It would be a close match, he thought. But he knew he and Ponton could take them.

As soon as the doors closed, Clouseau attacked.

By the time the elevator reached the twelfth floor, both of the Chinese men had been knocked out cold. Clouseau and Ponton stepped over the men's unconscious bodies and stepped out into a huge loft.

At the far end of the room, a man was bent over a desk, cutting something with a jeweler's saw. Xania stood nearby, watching him.

"Stop!" Clouseau cried, striding toward them. "Stop whatever you are doing. You are defenseless. We have already taken care of your thugs."

The jeweler put down his saw. "What thugs?"

"The thugs patrolling the building," said Clouseau.

"I don't have any thugs," said the jeweler, whose name was Sykorian.

"Of course you have thugs!" Clouseau cried.

"Why? The only stores in the building are a sunglasses shop and a Chinese take-out restaurant."

"Oh," said Clouseau, suddenly realizing his mistake. He leaned over to Ponton and whispered, "I think we owe someone an apology."

Ponton flashed his police badge at the jeweler. "What is it you are cutting?" he asked.

"Seven carats. A pink diamond. Clear." Sykorian held up the jewel.

"Clear? No flaw in the center resembling a lipping bist?" Clouseau asked.

"A *what*?" asked Sykorian, baffled by Clouseau's atrocious accent.

"A lipping bist!" said Clouseau.

"A leaping beast," Xania repeated, translating for Sykorian.

The jeweler shook his head. "It's clear. A gift

from the French minister of justice to his new mistress. I am to set it."

Ponton picked up the diamond and examined it. "It isn't the Pink Panther," he said.

"It is not the Pink Panther," Sykorian confirmed.

"And what are you doing here, sneaking around?" Clouseau asked, turning to Xania.

She held up a small clutch purse. The outside was studded with diamonds.

"This purse belonged to Josephine Baker," she said.

"Josephine Baker!" Clouseau and Ponton exclaimed in unison. They both fell into chairs, awestruck. Josephine Baker was like a goddess to the men of France.

"It was falling apart," Xania explained. "I had it studded with diamonds to use on stage at the presidential ball in Paris tomorrow."

"And why then did you arrange to see a black-market diamond-cutter?" Ponton wondered aloud.

"I didn't know he was black-market," Xania

replied. "My producer recommended him."

"Why did you not just tell me why you were coming?" Clouseau asked her.

"I can't be seen at a diamond dealer. Not after what happened," Xania said.

The phone rang. Sykorian scrambled to answer it, but Clouseau stopped him.

"I suspect that may be one of your mysterious clients now," he said. He picked up the phone. "Yes? . . . Yes, I am in charge of the phone bill," he told the person on the other end. "I'm somewhat happy with my service . . . no, I did not know that! Well, that is a bargain. I'll take the ten-year plan." Clouseau reached into his wallet, took out his credit card, and read off the number. Hanging up, he turned back to the others. "Whoo! I think I just got myself a pretty good deal," he exclaimed.

Just then, the phone rang again. Clouseau and Sykorian both reached for it.

"Let the machine get it," said Ponton.

The answering machine clicked on. "The 'animal' is out of its cage," the caller said mysteriously. "And since you are the world's greatest 'trainer,' in time it will come your way. Call me." *Click*. The caller hung up.

"Who was that?" Ponton asked.

"I do not know," said Sykorian. "Many people call here."

"It sounds to me that whoever that was has the Pink Panther," said Ponton.

Clouseau chuckled. "Ponton," he said, patting the younger man's cheek. "My sweet, silly Ponton. He was only talking about an animal that was out of its cage." He whipped around to point at the machine. "Don't leave town!" he commanded.

When they were finished, Clouseau and Ponton escorted Xania out of the building. Outside, they saw the sunglasses salesmen and the Chinese-food deliverymen being loaded into an ambulance on stretchers.

"When are you leaving the city?" Clouseau asked Xania.

"I am leaving tomorrow," she replied.

"Ah," said Clouseau. He pulled Ponton

aside. "I want to know what time her plane is leaving in the morning," he said.

"Why not just ask her?" said Ponton.

"Too obvious," said Clouseau. "I will need to pump her for information."

Just then, Xania stepped over to them. "Inspector, would you like to join me for dinner at the Waldorf?" she asked.

Seeing his opportunity, Clouseau agreed. "Of course, mademoiselle."

"Say, eight o'clock?" asked Xania.

"Eight o'clock," said Clouseau.

"Say, I don't know . . . my room on the second floor?" Xania suggested.

"I don't know, my room on the second floor," said Clouseau.

"I'll see you there," Xania said. She turned and walked off.

"It might be a trap," Ponton warned Clouseau when she was gone.

Clouseau smiled and watched Xania walk away. "But what a trap, Ponton," he said with a sigh. "What a trap."

Chapter 14

That evening, Clouseau met Xania in her luxurious hotel room. Xania lounged in her chair, sipping a glass of champagne. A flaming Mojito sat in front of Clouseau. The Inspector couldn't tear his eyes away from the gorgeous singer.

"Why?" Clouseau asked Xania, looking at her over the top of his fiery cocktail.

"Why what?" said Xania.

"Why were you being so elusive today?"

"I was afraid of Larocque . . . that he might be following me," Xania admitted.

"Larocque?" Clouseau asked, surprised.

"He had sent out word, threatening to kill anyone in possession of the Pink Panther. He believes it belongs to him," Xania said.

"And why would he follow you?" Clouseau wondered.

"I was in New York to see a diamond-cutter. He might draw the wrong conclusion," said Xania.

"You know," said Clouseau, staring into Xania's eyes, "a man sitting here in your private suite might draw the wrong conclusion, too."

"Or the right one," said Xania, meeting his gaze. "I have heard things about you."

"Really," said Clouseau, raising one eyebrow. He suavely leaned forward to sip from the straw in his drink. As he did so, his hair caught fire.

He didn't notice.

Excusing himself, Clouseau picked up his drink and slipped off the sofa. He backed down the hallway to the bathroom, still gazing at Xania.

Only when he looked in the mirror did Clouseau realize his hair was ablaze. Frantically, he tossed the flaming drink to the side and began to pat his burning hair.

At last, his hair stopped burning. Spotting a cozy bathrobe hanging on the door, Clouseau decided to change into something more comfortable. He took off his pants and shirt, then slipped the robe on over his underwear.

When he returned to the hotel room, Xania smiled at him.

"You like to make a girl wait," she said.

"All part of the plan," said Clouseau, sitting down next to Xania. He leaned in to kiss her. . . .

Suddenly the hotel fire alarm began to wail. "*FIRE ALERT,*" said a mechanical voice. "*EXIT THE BUILDING.*"

Clouseau and Xania sprang apart. Clouseau reached over to grab the robe.

"*DO NOT GRAB YOUR THINGS,*" the mechanical voice commanded. "*RUN. EXIT THE BUILDING.*"

Leaving the robe behind, Clouseau grabbed Xania's hand. They dashed out of the hotel together.

Out in the street, Clouseau and Xania saw dozens of other hotel guests who had been forced to flee their rooms as well. As they waited for the firemen to put out the blaze, Clouseau remembered why he'd come to see Xania in the first place.

"By the way, what time does your flight leave tomorrow?" he asked her.

"Ten A.M." she replied.

"Oh." Clouseau made a mental note of it. It might have taken all evening to get her to talk, Clouseau thought, but in the end, Inspector Clouseau always found out the truth.

The next morning, Clouseau showed up at the airport still wearing his T-shirt and boxer shorts. His pants and shirt had been lost in the fire in Xania's hotel room. As he waited to go through the security checkpoint, two airport guards pulled him aside, thinking he looked suspicious.

"This is an insult!" Clouseau cried, as they searched him. "I am Inspector Clouseau! I will report this to the highest person I know in France." He turned to the security guard and demanded, "What is your name?"

"Terry," the guard answered.

"Terry what?"

"Ahkeysauce," the guard said with a smirk.

"Well, Mr. Terry Ahkeysauce, I will report you. Ponton, take a photo of this!" he declared, handing Ponton his digital camera.

Clouseau posed with the guard as Ponton snapped their picture.

At last they made it on board the airplane. Xania was seated in first class. Clouseau started to sit down next to her, but the airline hostess stopped him.

"I'm sorry, your seat is not in first class," she told him.

"Not in first class?" Clouseau repeated. He turned to Ponton, who shrugged.

"Another insult," Clouseau growled.

"Come with me," said the hostess. She led Clouseau and Ponton into the next cabin. "You are here," she told Ponton.

"Trade with me," Clouseau begged him.

"Not permissible," the hostess said curtly.

She led Clouseau through the third cabin, then the fourth. Then the fifth, sixth, seventh, eighth, ninth, tenth, and eleventh cabins. Each cabin was shabbier than the last. The upholstery was stained and torn. The passengers looked scruffy. There was a weird smell.

In the twelfth cabin, panhandlers wandered through the aisles, asking for change. A few goats, pigs, and roosters were mixed in among the passengers.

A leper colony was living in the thirteenth cabin.

Finally, they came to the cabin at the very back of the plane. The dim, filthy room was bare except for a single wooden folding chair.

"Here you are," the hostess said to Clouseau, pointing to the chair, "and here's a menu. You should order now, because it could take hours."

Clouseau glanced quickly at the menu. "I'll have the sushi," he told the hostess.

As the plane took off, Clouseau settled back in his chair to wait for his sushi.

It was a long wait.

After several hours, the hostess returned with Clouseau's sushi. The fish stank. The rice was green with mold. It wasn't the hostess's fault—the sushi had been fresh when she left the galley. But the long, difficult journey through the airplane had taken its toll on Clouseau's dinner.

Clouseau, however, didn't notice.

"Do you want teriyaki sauce?" the hostess asked, handing the plate to him.

Clouseau's eyes narrowed as he recalled the security guard at the airport. "Oh, he will get his, all right," he snarled. Picking up a piece of sushi, he popped it into his mouth.

The hostess shrugged and left.

Clouseau gobbled down the rest of the sushi. With a satisfied sigh, he sat back in his chair and closed his eyes.

A moment later, his eyes flew open again. Had something been wrong with the sushi? he wondered. As if in reply, his stomach gurgled alarmingly. Clouseau leaped from his seat and hurried over to the restroom.

A sign on the door read OUT OF ORDER.

He hurried up to the next cabin and tried the restroom door. It was locked.

The restroom was locked in the next cabin, too. Clouseau jiggled the handle a few times. He was getting a little desperate.

In the tenth cabin, there was no restroom at all. In the ninth cabin it was locked. Clouseau began to run.

There was a line for the restroom in the eighth cabin. In the seventh cabin, the restroom was under construction. There was another line in the sixth cabin.

"Ah!" Clouseau cried, now completely desperate.

He tried the fifth, fourth, third, and second cabins. All the restrooms were locked. At last he was back in the first-class cabin. He began to pound on the door of the restroom, the door of the cockpit—any door he could find! He was desperate now.

"Let me in!" he screamed. "Let me in or I'm going to explode!"

Instantly, five plainclothes security officers sprang from their seats. They thought Clouseau was trying to hijack the plane! Grabbing the hysterical Inspector, they wrestled him to the floor.

Clouseau protested, but it was no use. The famed Inspector Clouseau, fighter of crime, was handcuffed like a criminal.

Chapter 15

Meanwhile, Dreyfus was on the verge of cracking the Gluant murder case. With his team of secret agents working around the clock, he had assembled all the evidence he needed. And it all pointed to one man.

"Gentlemen," Dreyfus said to the agents, who were once again assembled in his office, "meet Dr. Li How Pang, director of China's sports ministry." Dreyfus pointed to a blown-up photograph on the wall. "Here he is in China's VIP box just before Gluant was killed. Coincidentally, when Gluant was in Beijing, he had a number of meetings with the good Dr. Pang."

Dreyfus moved over to several enlarged

photos of Gluant in China. He picked up his collapsible pointer, but when he opened it, the pointer fell apart in his hands. Throwing the pointer aside in disgust, he used his finger to point at the photos. Two of the agents frowned disapprovingly.

Dreyfus ignored them. "In fact," he went on, "an examination of Pang's subsequent budget requisitions and Gluant's bank statements would indicate that they entered into an arrangement whereby Pang would send Gluant large sums of money diverted from the sports ministry's budget.

"Presumably, Gluant was to invest these sums on Pang's behalf. However . . ." Dreyfus continued, moving over to some enlarged images of Gluant's casino accounts, "Gluant, being a compulsive gambler, took the money and gambled it away, knowing full well that Pang couldn't press charges without exposing his own guilt—for which he would doubtless be executed by his government."

Dreyfus pointed at Pang's photo. "He had

the motive!" he declared. "He had the expertise! He had the opportunity!" He turned back to the agents. "Dr. Pang is in France for the presidential ball tonight. We will arrest him there for the murder of Yves Gluant."

The agents applauded. Just then, Renard hurried in, holding a newspaper.

"Have you seen this?" he asked, thrusting the paper in front of Dreyfus. The headline read: CLOUSEAU EZ ARRESTED AT ZEE AIRPORT.

Dreyfus could barely contain his glee. He tried to hide his grin. "This is a horrible tragedy," he said, the corners of his mouth twitching. At last, he thought, Inspector Clouseau has been cut down to size. And now that Dreyfus had solved Gluant's murder, nothing stood between him and the Medal of Honor.

Just then, the police car carrying Clouseau arrived at the Palais de la Justice. Dreyfus and Renard watched from the balcony as the handcuffed inspector was led inside.

"Well, so much for the heroic Inspector Clouseau," Dreyfus said, letting out a little chuckle. "Take me to him."

In the interrogation room, Clouseau sat squinting under the harsh lights, where only days before he himself had been questioning other suspects. Dreyfus, Renard, Ponton, and several other officers surrounded him.

"What was going to explode?" Dreyfus asked Clouseau.

"Nothing," said Clouseau, embarrassed.

"What was going to explode?" Dreyfus repeated, louder.

"I'm not going to tell you," Clouseau said in a little-boy voice.

"What was going to explode?" Dreyfus yelled at him.

"I'm not going to tell you," Clouseau said again.

"Well, then, Clouseau, it's a glorious day for France," Dreyfus gloated, "because a stupid idiot named Clouseau is going to be stripped of his rank, while I take over his case."

"You have a second man named Clouseau?" Clouseau asked, surprised.

Dreyfus shook his head in disgust. "You are incompetent," he spat.

"I have been promoted?" said Clouseau.

Dreyfus stared at him. "What?"

"I have been promoted to incompetent?" Clouseau stood up from his chair. "From now on, everyone will address me as In-COMP-e-taunt!" he declared.

Dreyfus had had enough. "Everybody out!" he ordered. "Enough embarrassment for the Inspector. I want to talk to him alone."

The other police officers shuffled out. Ponton and Renard stayed behind.

"Understand something, Clouseau," Dreyfus said when they were gone. "When I made you an inspector, it was not because I thought you had any value as a detective. It was because I believed you to be the stupidest policeman in all of France. A total idiot."

Clouseau looked at him, confused. "An idiot?"

"Yes." Dreyfus nodded. "A hopeless, deluded idiot."

As Dreyfus spoke, Clouseau seemed to shrink. "Then I was not promoted for my merits?" he asked in a tiny voice.

"Name one," Dreyfus retorted. "I only made you an inspector because I wanted someone who would quietly get nowhere until I was ready to take over the case myself!"

His knees weakening, Clouseau sank into the chair. "My charm?" he managed to say.

"What?"

"You said to name one."

"You can't even conduct a normal conversation!" Dreyfus cried.

"I was trying to catch a killer," Clouseau told him.

"You were trying to become a hero," Dreyfus retorted. "Well, you'll now be stripped of your rank, ridiculed in the media, and I'll be done with you. Now, if you'll excuse me, I have to prepare for the arrest that will catapult me to the National Assembly. Good-bye, Clouseau." He turned to leave.

"Shall we lock him up?" Renard asked, ready

to handcuff Clouseau and take him away.

Dreyfus glanced back at the deflated Clouseau. "Look at him," he sneered. "He is finished. Let him go back home to his obscurity."

Dreyfus and Renard left the room, leaving Clouseau to stare into space, utterly defeated.

Chapter 16

Later that afternoon, Ponton drove Clouseau back to his apartment.

"I am sorry, Inspector," Ponton said, as Clouseau got out of the car. He stood to shake Clouseau's hand. "I had no idea you were being used."

"I am a fool, Ponton," Clouseau replied. "And if I ever made you look foolish, I am sorry."

"It was an honor serving under you, sir," said Ponton.

Clouseau smiled sadly. Raising his arm, he gave Ponton a feeble karate chop. This time, Ponton let it land.

Then, his shoulders sagging, Clouseau turned and walked into his apartment.

That evening, Clouseau watched himself being dragged in handcuffs into the Palais de la Justice on the evening news. The newscast cut to an interview with Inspector Dreyfus.

"I am pleased to say that I am now taking over the Pink Panther investigation, and that an arrest is imminent," Dreyfus declared.

"The coroner has announced that Bizu was killed by a perfect shot to the occipital lobe," the TV news anchor reported. "Any comments?"

Dreyfus dismissed it with a wave of his hand. "Unimportant," he said.

"The occipital lobe," Clouseau murmured, watching. It was ringing a bell in the back of his mind. "The occipital lobe."

But, he reminded himself, this was no longer his case. With a sigh, Clouseau shut off the television. Spotting his digital camera on the desk, he picked it up and followed the instructions in the camera's manual to view the pictures.

Clouseau glanced through several pictures of himself and Ponton in New York City. When he came to the photo of himself being frisked at the airport, Clouseau paused.

"I will still report this little incident," he promised himself.

Clouseau looked closer at the photograph. In the background, he saw Xania standing by the X-ray machine at the security checkpoint.

"You will not love me now, will you, Xania?" he said sadly.

Just then, something caught his attention. He squinted at the tiny photo.

"Hmmm," said Clouseau. Moving over to his computer, he flipped through the instruction manual until he found the page labeled HOW TO ENLARGE A PHOTO.

Several mouse clicks later, Clouseau's eyes widened. He dashed to the phone and dialed a number. "Ponton!" he cried. "Get over here immediately!"

Hanging up, he dialed another number. "Nicole," he said when she answered, "on your way to the ball tonight, go to my office; bring me the vinyl bag marked PRESIDENTIAL PALACE. I will meet you there. Hurry!"

Moments later, Ponton pulled up in front of Clouseau's apartment. Clouseau scrambled into the passenger seat. "Ponton, we must get to the presidential palace immediately!" he cried.

"If I drive fast, will that bother you?" Ponton asked, starting the engine.

"Are you kidding? Let's see what this baby can . . . *ahhh*!" Ponton hit the gas pedal, and the car lurched forward, sending Clouseau flying out the back. At the last moment he grabbed on to the back window. The car sped down the road with Clouseau flapping behind it like a flag.

"What is this all about?" Ponton yelled back to him.

"Gluant and Bizu were killed by the same person, and I believe the killer will strike again tonight," Clouseau shouted.

"But Bizu was killed by a rifle," Ponton yelled. "And Gluant by a poison Chinese dart."

"Sometimes I like steak, and sometimes I like

chicken," Clouseau replied. "The killer does not want us to think he is the same man. The question to ask now is not 'How were the two murders different?' but 'What did the dead men have in common?'"

"Xania?" Ponton guessed.

"Exactly."

"She killed them?"

"No, Ponton!" cried Clouseau. "She is the next victim!"

Chapter 17

The presidential palace bustled with activity as everyone prepared for the ball. Dressed in a tuxedo, Dreyfus stood at the entryway, going over the guest list with the security chief.

"Ah, yes, Clouseau's name should be crossed off the list," Dreyfus said. "He has been humiliated. He should not be allowed in affairs of the state."

"And what about all the reporters who will want in?" the security chief asked.

"When the time is right, let them pour in," Dreyfus said. He wanted every news team in France to be there to witness his capture of Gluant's killer.

It was dark by the time Clouseau and Ponton arrived at the presidential palace. They parked the car and hurried to the main entrance, where a pretty woman was taking tickets. She ran her finger down a list, checking for their names.

"I'm sorry, but your name is not on the list," she told Clouseau.

"Dreyfus must have made sure you can't get in," Ponton whispered to him.

"Let me try to charm her," Clouseau whispered back. He leaned over and whispered something in the ticket-taker's ear.

"Ewww!" she cried. Disgusted, she ran off. Immediately, two large guards stepped in, blocking the entrance.

Clouseau signaled for Ponton to retreat. They walked back down the stairs to look for another way in.

Just then, they heard what sounded like a bird's call. Clouseau looked around and saw Nicole signaling to them from behind the building.

They ran over to her.

"Inspector, here is your bag," she said, handing him the satchel she'd brought from his office. "Plus, I thought you might need these—the architectural plans of the presidential palace."

"Ah. Good work," said Clouseau.

"What is it?" Ponton asked, peering at the bag.

"Camouflage."

Ponton raised his eyebrows. "You surprise me, Inspector."

"Get used to it, Ponton. With me, surprises are rarely unexpected," replied Clouseau. Turning back to Nicole, he added, "Wish us luck."

"You don't need luck," she replied. "You are Inspector Clouseau."

"Yes, I am," Clouseau agreed. "But what about him?" He jerked his thumb at Ponton.

"Go!" Nicole urged them.

"Yes, we must. Nicole, one thing," Clouseau added. He looked at her with a romantic twinkle in his eye, noticing how radiant she looked in her ball gown. Walking over to her, he removed her glasses. "You look beautiful without your glasses," he told her.

"Why, thank you, Inspector," Nicole replied, blushing slightly. Half blind, she staggered off in the direction of the palace door and stumbled into the bushes.

Inside the presidential palace, the ball was in full swing. Men in tuxedos and women in elegant gowns mingled in the elegant ballroom, sipping champagne. The French president chatted with Monsieur Clochard, while in the middle of the room Dr. Pang moved through the crowd, surrounded by his bodyguards. Dreyfus watched them like a hawk.

"Chief Inspector," the security chief said, suddenly walking up to Dreyfus, "our guards have reported the sighting of Inspector Clouseau."

"I know what he's up to. He's going to try to make the arrest himself," Dreyfus snarled. "If you see Clouseau, put him in cuffs for trespassing, and parade him through the party," he told the chief.

The security chief nodded and murmured something into the microphone attached to his lapel. Immediately, all of the security guards in the room went on the alert.

When the security chief was gone, Dreyfus whispered to Renard, "Pang's just entered the room." He checked his watch. "We'll take him in ten minutes."

In a lavish dressing room just off the ballroom, Xania was getting ready to go onstage. She sat before a large mirror, brushing makeup onto her face.

As she gazed into the mirror, Xania saw the door open behind her. Larocque and Huang entered the room. Xania put down her makeup brush.

"Well, aren't we pretty?" Larocque said, walking over to her.

Xania raised her chin and glared at him. *"We?"* she replied coldly.

"I know you killed Gluant," Larocque said, his smooth voice changing to a snarl.

"Don't be ridiculous," Xania snapped.

"Oh, believe me, I don't care," Larocque assured her. "I hated him. But the ring belongs to me."

"But I don't have the stupid ring," Xania told him. "And even if I did, why would it belong to you?"

"Because I want it. And I always get what I want. And if I don't get what I want," he added, "ugly things could happen to a very pretty girl." He reached out and touched her cheek. "Beauty is so fragile, don't you think?"

He gave Xania a sinister smile. Xania stared back at him, her eyes filled with fear.

Just then, the lights in the presidential ballroom dimmed. It was time for Xania to go onstage. Brushing past Larocque and Huang, she hurried out of the dressing room.

In the ballroom, the crowd applauded loudly as Xania appeared onstage. Silhouetted behind a white curtain, she opened her diamond-studded handbag, reached for a lipstick, and dabbed some on her lips. Then the curtain rose, and Xania began to sing.

At the far edge of the room, opposite the stage, there was a slight movement near the floral curtains that framed the ballroom's tall windows. Only the keenest eye could have made out the shape of Inspector Clouseau pressed against the wall. Dressed in a skintight bodysuit that perfectly matched the curtains, he was almost completely invisible.

He edged along the curtain until he came to the marble wall, then flipped over. The back of his suit matched the marble exactly. Reaching out for the next curtain, Clouseau flipped himself again. Now, once more, he matched the curtains.

In this way, Clouseau flip-flopped his way along the wall. When he was halfway down the room, Ponton entered. Dressed in a bodysuit exactly like Clouseau's, he began to flip himself along the wall, too.

Finally, they reached an open door and

simultaneously dashed through it.

Out in the hallway, Ponton and Clouseau stripped off their camouflage outfits. Underneath, they both wore tight black suits with masks.

Suddenly, they heard a shuffling overhead.

"Footsteps!" cried Clouseau, listening carefully. They looked up just in time to see a black-suited figure dash into a dark stairwell.

Clouseau and Ponton chased after him. They raced up one stairwell and down another, but they couldn't tell which way he had gone.

As they ran, Clouseau blundered into one wall after another.

"Did you see where he went?" Ponton asked.

"Frankly, I am not seeing too well out of this outfit," replied Clouseau, smacking into another wall.

Ponton looked him over. "It looks good on you," he said.

"You think?" asked Clouseau, flattered.

Scrambling up another flight of stairs, they came out in an upstairs hallway, which overlooked the grand ballroom.

"Inspector, look!" exclaimed Ponton. He pointed up at the ceiling. In one of the skylights, they saw a crossbow, which was aimed directly into the ballroom.

"There could be a million harmless explanations for a crossbow being pointed into a room of French people, but we can take no chances," Clouseau said. "Come on!"

"This way!" said Ponton, pointing to a small window leading out to the roof.

They squeezed through the window. On the rooftop the killer was kneeling over the skylight, his finger on the crossbow's trigger. As Clouseau and Ponton burst out onto the roof, he turned, startled.

"The jeeg is erp," Clouseau told him.

"What?" said the killer.

"The jeeg is erp," Clouseau repeated.

"The jeeg?" said the killer, baffled by Clouseau's accent.

"Yes, it's erp," Clouseau told him. Just then, the killer dropped the crossbow and fled.

Chapter 18

Back in the ballroom, Xania's song was almost over. Dreyfus checked his watch. It was time for his plan.

"Now we make the arrest," he whispered. He signaled to the secret agents stationed around the room. Stealthily, they began to move forward.

As Xania finished the song, the crowd applauded. Dreyfus nodded to the security chief, who suddenly threw open the doors to the ballroom. A mob of reporters rushed into the room.

"Now!" screamed Dreyfus.

At once, the secret agents pulled out their

weapons. They surrounded the startled Dr. Pang and his men.

Dreyfus stepped forward. "Well, Dr. Pang, you thought you could come here and make a mockery of the French police," he said. "In the name of the statutes and laws of the great nation of France, I arrest you for the murder of Yves Gluant!"

The crowd in the room gasped. The room exploded with flashes of light as the news crews snapped pictures.

Just then, there was a commotion on the landing above. The killer burst into the room, with Ponton and Clouseau right behind him.

"Clouseau! Arrest him!" Dreyfus cried. He looked back and forth between the three masked figures. "Which one is he?" he added. They all looked exactly alike.

The first black-suited man leaped onto the banister and slid down it. The second one followed right behind him. Then the third man leaped onto the banister—and promptly plummeted over the ledge.

"Ahhhh!" he cried as he fell to the floor.

"That would be him," said Dreyfus.

Thump. Clouseau landed right on top of the killer, knocking him down. Clouseau leaped to his feet. "In the name of the statutes and laws of the great nation of France," he declared, "I arrest you for the murder of Yves Gluant, Yuri, the trainer who trains!"

Clouseau ripped off the mask covering the killer's face, revealing Yuri, the trainer for the French soccer team.

Again, the crowd gasped. The news crews left Dreyfus and rushed over to Clouseau.

"Gluant was *nothing*!" Yuri snarled bitterly, as camera shutters clicked all around him. "*I* drew up the plays! *I* designed the offense! He takes credit for the brilliant French defense, which I gave him! He takes it and treats me like I'm dead. Fine. Now *he's* dead—from Chinese poison."

Ponton turned to Clouseau, his eyes wide. "But what made you think it was him?" he asked.

"Ponton, think back. You were there," said

Clouseau. He reminded Ponton of Mrs. Yu, the Chinese woman they had interrogated. If Ponton had understood Chinese, as Clouseau did, he would have remembered the clue she'd given them. "Why do you bother me?" the harassed woman had cried. "Why did you bring me down here? I'm busy! The soccer player was killed with Chinese poison. You should look for soccer trainers. They are required to have a knowledge of Chinese herbs!"

"She was right," Clouseau explained to Ponton. "Statute 87223: 'Every trainer of the national soccer team must have a knowledge of Chinese herbs.' This made it easy for him to murder Gluant."

"And Bizu?" asked a reporter.

"Simple," said Clouseau. "Bizu had often heard Yuri's rants against Gluant. So Bizu black-mailed Yuri and got himself killed. A stunning shot to the head," Clouseau reminded every-one, "burrowing deeply into the occipital lobe."

"But Yuri is a trainer," Dreyfus protested, furious that Clouseau was once again getting all the attention. "That shot was made by an expert."

"Correct!" Clouseau exclaimed. "Russian Army statute 611. All members must be excellent marksmen and understand the location of the occipital lobe."

Yuri scowled. He glanced over at Xania.

"Yes, Yuri," Clouseau said, reading the killer's thoughts. "She is still alive. But you hated her. You helped her when she was struggling, but she went with Bizu and then Gluant and treated you like you were nothing. And that's why you were trying to kill her. The case is closed."

Dreyfus pushed his way through the crowd and stormed up to Clouseau. "Thank you for carrying out my instructions, Inspector Clouseau," he declared, still hoping to take the credit for the killer's arrest. He turned to Yuri. "Now, hand over the diamond," he demanded.

"What do I care about a stinking diamond?" Yuri said, glowering. "It is nothing to me!"

"He does not have the diamond," Clouseau said calmly.

"He does not have the diamond? The murderer does not have the diamond?" Dreyfus couldn't believe what he was hearing.

"No," said Clouseau.

"Then where is the diamond?" Dreyfus demanded.

Clouseau walked over to Xania. "There!" he cried. "In her purse."

The crowd gasped.

"Let me see," said Dreyfus. Grabbing Xania's purse, he unceremoniously dumped its contents out onto a table. A tube of lipstick fell out, along with a compact, a ticket stub, and some change—but no Pink Panther.

"Sorry, Clouseau, no diamond," Dreyfus said smugly.

Clouseau walked over and picked up the purse. Taking out a small pocketknife, he carefully sliced open the lining. There, nestled in the silk, was the Pink Panther diamond.

"Ooooh!" cried the crowd in unison. Flashbulbs popped all around them.

"Yes, I have it," Xania admitted. "After

Gluant came to me on the day of the game, he said he'd decided to stop cheating on me. Then he asked me to marry him and put the ring into my hands.

"After he was killed," Xania went on, "I thought if I came forward with the ring, everyone would think *I* did it."

"Gluant worked for the nation of France," Dreyfus blustered, still trying to claim some glory for himself. "Therefore, I claim that ring for the state of France."

Clouseau shook his head. "I am sorry, Chief Inspector," he said, "but according to civil statute 106, '*If a citizen dies prior to marriage, his fiancée has the right to claim ownership of the token, regardless of association with the State.*' Xania," he said, turning to the singer, "you may keep the Pink Panther."

"But Inspector, how did you know she had it?" asked Ponton.

"It was simple, Ponton. I was looking at the photograph of myself at the checkpoint," Clouseau explained. "Something caught my eye: Xania's purse, passing through the X-ray machine. I enlarged the photo. In the purse was the Pink Panther."

"Bravo!" a reporter yelled.

"Bravo, Clouseau!" another reporter echoed.

Clouseau looked around, surprised and pleased, as more people took up the chant. Renard could barely restrain the seething Dreyfus, as the entire ballroom rang with the cry:

"Bravo, Clouseau!"